A Novella By
Tiffany Gilbert

Iman and Miracle: Love Conquers All
Copyright © 2018 by Tiffany Gilbert
Published by Boss Chic Empire Presents.

All rights reserved this book is a work of fiction. Names, characters, places, and incidents either are the product of author's imagination or are use fictiously and are not to be construed as real. Any resemblance to actual personals, living or dead, business establishments, events, or locales or, is entirely coincidental. No portion of this book may be used or reproduced in any manner whatsoever without writer permission except in the case of brief quotations embodied in critical articles and reviews.

Table of Contents

ACKNOWLEDGEMENTS 4
CHAPTER ONE 7
CHAPTER TWO 11
CHAPTER THREE 17
CHAPTER FOUR 21
CHAPTER FIVE 29
CHAPTER SIX 34
CHAPTER SEVEN 38
CHAPTER EIGHT 42
CHAPTER NINE 61
CHAPTER TEN 81
CHAPTER ELEVEN 91
CHAPTER TWELVE 100
COMING SOON 118
FROM 118
TIFFANY GILBERT 118
TIFFANY GILBERT 119
INTRODUCTION 120
CHAPTER ONE 122
CHAPTER TWO 127
CHAPTER THREE 136

Acknowledgements

I would like to first give all thanks to my father the man above God without God giving me this talent to be able to write books and put my words together I wouldn't be the author I am today. I would also like to thank my parents Martha (My M-Dot) and Leroy (My Bo) because I wouldn't even be here today without them.

My parents gave me life and raised me to be the Woman I have become today so I thank them for allowing me to go off and achieve my goals. My parents set me up and taught me that I can be and do anything life that I want as long as I put my best foot first. I would love to thank My King, My Roc, Roc, Roc, My Husband Mr. Deshawn Gilbert for always standing by my side and always believing in me and telling me I can do it. My husband told me don't give up and When I first started writing nine years ago my husband was right there with me helping me I love my husband for always being there your my Roc.

I would like to thank my siblings my two big sisters Lisa and Elizabeth they help raise me and treated me like they own child. My sisters have always been there from the beginning and haven't left my side yet and I love them for that. I would love to thank my Niece's (Laquitia, Dominique (Domo), Aubree and Kenya and My Nephews Alonzo (Zo) and Carlos (Los) we grew up like siblings yeah I know and I'm the auntie. I love my babies they been right here from the start kicking up dust with me where would I be without them. I would love to give out a Major shout out My Publisher Shantay when I wanted to give up writing after every storm I had been through she gave me a chance.

Shantay stayed up late nights teaching me the ropes of Editing and making sure I understood everything about writing a book. I can't thank you enough for all you have done. Boss Chic is everything it is because of you Shantay love you girl.

I would like to shout out my pen sisters Erika and Kim you two have embraced me and took me in as y'all sisters and I thank you Kim for the early morning conversations after I been up all night writing and Erika for all the laughs and trying to help me understand this writing thing I love both of y'all. I would like to also thank My god parents Mrs. Betty Harris may you rest in peace I love and miss you. Mrs. Faye I love you mother your always there for me and always there to support me no matter what. Mr. and Mrs. Renfroe I've known you both half of my life and its not one time I can't recall when I call that either you haven't answered I love you both. I would like to thank My God Sister's Channell (Nellie) my oldest friend from preschool you never been fake and you always there to have my back I know for a doubt I can call you anytime and you going to always be there. Tracey, Niqua, Rell you three heffas are always down for me no matter what and I thank and love y'all. I would like to thank my bff Cheyenne girl you are truly crazy and I love you I've known you since middle school and never have you turned your back on me. I would like to thank Latoya my bestest and my nieces Raine, Annia and Raven y'all family took me in six years ago and haven't turned y'all back yet and I love y'all. Last and not least I would love to thank all my supporters and my readers for ever picking up my books and reading them and leaving reviews without y'all I wouldn't even be an author. I would love to thank my HATERS because of Y'all I'M STILL STANDING. HI HATER, BYE HATER.

Chapter One

The introduction of Miracle and Iman

Waking up this morning was really a task. I didn't want to get out of my plush, king size bed, but I had to since there was a business I needed to run. I had everything I wanted in life except the right man. My ex, Cameron, had left me salty and I had vowed to never give another nigga my all again. My name is Miracle Lanay Captains, I am twenty-five years old, born and raised in the Warren and Connors projects. I knew what it meant to have nothing, so I did my best to get to where I was today with the help of my ex. Looking at my phone ring as I got out of bed, it was my best friend Sasha, who was also my business partner. Sending her a text, I let her know I was getting in the shower and I'd be at the boutique no later than an hour.

Looking in the mirror, I must admit, I was a bad-ass bitch. All my sexiness stood at 5'5, weighing one hundred and forty pounds. I had blonde highlights in my hair that reached the middle of my back. I drove these niggas in Detroit crazy. They couldn't get enough of Mrs. Miracle, but I needed my king. He had to be rough around the edges, a savage, and know how to treat Mrs. Kitty right. Turning on Tamar Braxton's new CD *Bluebird Of Happiness*, I let her album play. I loved Tamar.

7

Adjusting the water for my shower to the right temperature, I grabbed my cucumber melon shower gel, making sure I smelled good. Hitting all the important spots on my body had me feeling good and sexy. It had been roughly six months since Mrs. Kitty had been touched. Rubbing in between my legs, pinching my nipples, I could feel myself coming close to an orgasm. As soon as I let loose, I smiled and finished washing myself off. Drying off, I went into my room, grabbed my lotion and rubbed my body down. It was cold as hell in Detroit, and I hated to be ashy.

I wanted to be comfortable today, so I went for my black Balmain jeans, a Gucci sweater, and Gucci loafers for the day. Picking out the perfect purse to match my outfit because I had to be the best dressed, I snatched my keys from the countertop, secured the house alarm and hit the alarm to my 2018 Range Rover. Once I got in, I set my pretty Gucci bag on the passenger seat. Pulling out of the driveway, making sure I kept my eyes on the road, I decided to stop by Starbucks to get coffee and donuts for my staff and I. Walking into the coffee shop, I stood in line and was getting ready to order when this rude-ass nigga started ordering his coffee.

"Yeah, let me get a vanilla cap with three sugars and extra vanilla."

"Excuse me, I'm next in line!" I said with an attitude.

This was why I couldn't stand niggas in Detroit: they thought they ran something. I didn't give a damn how much money these niggas thought they had or who they thought they were. This was why I was single. Niggas in Detroit didn't have any respect.

"My bad, ma, but I'm in a hurry," he said, turning around.

My panties got so moist. This nigga was all kinds of fine but looking good didn't get it with me. Standing at 5'8, he had perfect, golden skin with a goatee and a low-cut fade. I could see the tats all over his neck, which led me to believe that he might have tats all over his body, but since he had on a long sleeve shirt, I couldn't tell. I could tell by the sound of his voice that he could get me out of my panties. These were the kind of niggas I needed to stay away from.

"Nigga, I am not your ma, first off, and I don't care if you're in a hurry. I was in line and your rude ass cut in front of me like you the only person who has shit to do. I know your mama taught you some respect and manners, so next time, use them."

I stood with my hands on my hips, ready to slap the fuck out of him because he thought it was OK to disrespect women.

"Can you hurry the fuck up? I am already late and standing here conversing with your ass is not going to get me to my boutique any quicker."

"That would be $5.48," said the cashier. He gave the cashier a fifty-dollar bill. "Sorry, sir, we don't take bills over twenty dollars."

"It's OK, pay for whatever this young lady wants, and you can keep the change."

Who the fuck does he think he's winking his eye at? I didn't think that shit was amusing. That was why I didn't deal with these Detroit niggas. Sticking my middle finger up at his cocky ass, he left, and I placed my order and paid for my own stuff because I didn't want his money and I didn't want him to think it was that easy. I hurried and got my order and left.

Walking into the boutique an hour and a half later, I was so pissed. I walked right into my office that I shared with Sasha and sat down to check numbers and order some new merchandise for the store.

"Heffa, I didn't know you were here," Sasha said, walking into the office.

"Yeah, I have been here for almost twenty minutes. My bad for being late. This rude, fine-ass nigga cut me off while I was at Starbucks." Sasha was cracking up laughing at me because she knew I couldn't stand rude-ass niggas and hated people.

"I know damn well you're not laughing while I was out getting your greedy ass breakfast," I said.

Sasha said, "Aww, boo, thank you. Anyhow, did you get the guy's name?"

"Hell no, fuck that rude-ass bastard!"

Sasha took that as her cue to leave and greet customers because she knew I didn't want to argue. I kept my ass in the office because I wasn't in the mood. Working through the day, I ordered lunch for the workers instead of going out. We had to prep for our new inventory for the spring that we were going to have coming in.

Chapter Two

Iman

I am Iman Juan Harris, thirty years old, born and raised on the Eastside of Detroit. I am what you call the King of the D. I run Detroit. There's nothing you can do in my city, and I don't know about it. I raised myself; my moms and pops were crack heads. I couldn't talk about them because I sold their asses the same drugs they used. I had no heart and didn't give a fuck about anybody, but my team, The Get Money Boys.

I didn't have a main bitch, so whenever I wanted to get my dick wet, I just hit one of these bitches I wanted to deal with. Aside from my illegal operation, I owned a barber shop, a club, and a bar and grill. I was thinking about what I wanted to do next. A nigga had it all, I was just ready to settle down. Thinking about little mama I saw earlier in the coffee shop this morning had me thinking about making her mine and giving her my last name. I hadn't been this comfortable with a bitch since my ex, Janay. Thinking about that rat bitch made me mad all over again. I had given this bitch the world just for this bitch to run off with the next nigga like I wasn't the king of the city. I was going to put my ears to the street and find out who she was.

Going into the warehouse, I saw all my niggas sitting around the table for our monthly meeting. We needed to figure out how to expand. I was ready to take over another city. You know what they say, the more money, the more problems. I was ready to settle down and live life with the right woman by my side.

"I think we're ready to expand our business and take over some more cities."

"I'm thinking Atlanta," my right-hand man, Brian, said.

"I'm with you, Iman. I mean, we already got Detroit on lock; now we need to lock down something else."

"OK, what we're going to do is send some of our best workers down there to scope out things, set things up and report back to us. Don't make a move unless B or I tell you to. Are we clear?" Everyone agreed.

B and I were still sitting at the table. I started telling him about the mystery girl, and he told me he was going to check into it, and he would get back with me later. I dapped him up and left out to head home to take a nap. On the way home, I had a taste for Benihana's rice and some chicken. After picking up my food, I stopped by the store to grab a couple of blunts. I was about to chill because all of my business had been taken care of and it was only four PM, so I was on good timing.

Hopefully, B got that information for me soon because shorty was on my mind hard. I think I had found love. You know what they say, love conquers all. I hoped she loved me for the savage I am. Pulling up into my driveway, the first thing I spotted was my ex Janay's car. I pinched the bridge of my nose. I didn't know what she wanted or why she was here, but she had five seconds to get the fuck away from my house. I grabbed my food and got out the car. As I approached, she stepped out her BMW, the car I had gotten her for her twenty-ninth birthday last year.

Janay started to speak instantly. "Iman, baby, can we talk?"

"Janay, you better go talk to that nigga Quincy. What we had is over, and I don't have anything to say to your bitch ass. Get the fuck away from my house before I put a bullet in your ass like I should have done when I found out you were cheating. Consider yourself blessed to still be alive."

"Mani, I still love you, and I am so sorry," she cried, calling me the nickname she had given me. "I never meant to cheat. You were out here cheating and carrying on like you didn't have a woman at home. You treated me like shit, and I carried your baby."

"Janay, our son is dead. Please just go. I don't have time to talk to your ass today. When I want some pussy, I know how to reach you, but until then, get the fuck away from my house and don't come back!"

She looked at me, and I almost felt sorry for her ass, but I didn't. She had made her bed, and now she must lay in it. She got in her car, and I went into my house, kicking off my shoes. I went into my theater room and kicked back, watching *Paid In Full,* one of my favorite movies. I must have dozed off because when I woke up, it was seven PM, and I had missed calls and messages from B. He told me he had found out about little mama and her name was Miracle Captains, she was twenty-five years old and owned a boutique in Eastland Mall with her friend, Sasha. B also told me he was going out with Sasha. I wondered why I had never met Miss Miracle. B told me she was single and he gave me her number and address. I thanked my nigga and told him I'd holler at him later. I also had a text message from Janay pleading her case again. I blocked that bitch. I knew she was going to be a problem. She was getting on my damn nerves. Why couldn't she just leave me alone? I got up, threw my containers away, rolled a blunt, and went to the bathroom to wash my face and brush my teeth. Deciding to take a shower and a shit, I decided since I wasn't doing anything, I was going to text my future wife.

Me: Hey, li'l mama.

Future wife: Who the fuck is this?

Me: Your future husband. You didn't think you were going to get away from me that easy, did you?

Future wife: Husband! Nigga, I'm single as a dollar bill, so who the fuck is this playing on my phone?

Me: This is Iman, the sexy nigga from the coffee shop this morning.

Future wife: Iman, nigga, how da fuck you get my number? Are you stalking me? Do I need to call the police on your ass?

Me: Look, be ready at 9. I'll be there to pick you up, OK? And wear something sexy, li'l mama.

Future wife: Iman or whoever the fuck you are, you got me fucked up. I'm not going anywhere with you, and you don't know where I lay my head. Goodbye.

Me: You must don't know, I'm a king, I know everything. I run this city, Miss Miracle. I'll see you at 9 PM.

I chuckled after reading her last text about our date and got into the shower. Stepping out of the shower, drying off, and going into my walk-in closet, I decided to keep it simple. I threw on a nice jogging fit and my red Jordan 11s. I was a good-looking nigga. Brown-skinned, 360s, and hazel-brown eyes. No wonder all the bitches' panties stayed wet, but I was willing to put all these hoes to the side and make Miracle my one and only.

Jumping into my BMW 8 series, I placed Miracle's address into my GPS, so I could pick her up. Turned out she stayed a few blocks away from me in Sterling Heights in a condo. Pulling up to her house and getting out, I knocked on the door. I had to check my attire when she opened the door in a Nike jogging suit and the same damn red Jordan11s. I had to smile; she must have been thinking about. Baby girl looked damn good, and I was ready to taste that pussy.

Rolling her eyes and grabbing her purse, she locked the door without saying hello or anything.

"Hello," I said to her.

"Yeah, whatever. Hey, Iman. Let's hurry up, I got work tomorrow. Where are we going? Why are you dressed like me? Damn."

"I was dressed first, lady. Sit back and ride, we're going to enjoy our night."

Chapter Three

First Date

I was impressed as I sat back in Iman's car. I didn't know how he had gotten my information. He had my pussy all wet thinking about how he had tried to make boss moves. I wondered what it was about this man. She wanted to give him a try because she had been single for too long. As long as he didn't have anything to hide and wasn't on any bullshit, she was cool. Valentine's Day was next month, who said you couldn't fall in love on sight? She couldn't keep her eyes off him while he drove. He smiled at her, and she couldn't help but let her guard down a little as she smiled back.

She texted Sasha and let her know who she was with, and she said she already knew she was with Iman. She wondered how the fuck she knew who she was with. She had to explain herself.

Iman couldn't help but keep his eyes on her. He thought she was beautiful, even her feisty attitude. He had to have her, and if things went well, he wouldn't be single for Valentine's Day.

Iman pulled up to the airport and parked, then tapped Miracle. She woke up and adjusted herself in the chair.

"Umm, Iman, why are we at the airport?" He chuckled, got out and walked around and opened her door.

"Come on, we 'bout to take a little trip. Don't worry, you will be back by Monday morning. Everything is already arranged. Let a nigga show you the world and give you the world."

She just smiled and got out. "But, Iman, I don't have any clothes with me."

He smiled and said, "With me, we don't pack clothes, we shop when we touch down."

She grabbed his hand, and they got on the jet.

He asked her, "What do you want to drink and eat?"

She asked, "Where is the bathroom?" He pointed down the hall.

"I want a shot of Patrón with a touch of lime and pineapple and get me some food."

He smiled and got her whatever she wanted.

When she got in the bathroom, she couldn't believe she was on a date with the same nigga she had just cursed out hours ago. She couldn't believe she was on a plane with him going out of town. Then, on top of that, when she got back, she was going to curse Sasha's ass out. She washed her hands and came out. When she got back to her seat, her drink and food were there already. Iman was on the phone, barking orders, so she just sat across from him, sipped her drink and watched how he moved like a boss. She thought he was sexy and she wanted him in the worst way. Once he noticed her in front of him, he told B he was going to be out of town for a few days and to take care of everything and let him know if he was needed.

He smiled at her and jumped right into the questions. "How come you single?"

She took a sip of her drink and thought about how to answer that question. "Well, to be honest, Iman, I've been single for six months. My ex and I broke up, and I pretty much put my mind in another space and got in my bag so I could focus on my business. I vowed to never allow another man to get in my mind and take control of my heart and soul and do me wrong again."

She asked, "So, why are you single?"

He chuckled. "Long story short, I caught my ex cheating on me after I gave her the world and she did me dirty."

She said, "Damn, Iman, I am sorry to hear that. So, what do you do for a living, Iman?"

He knew this question was coming. He wasn't afraid of what he did for a living, he just didn't know if he could trust her. Something in his heart told him to just be honest and let her know.

"I own a few businesses, but I also do some illegal things as well."

He looked at her to catch her facial expression.

He said to her, "Look, I want to do things differently with you because you have me feeling some kind of way. I need to be honest and go with my gut and just trust you."

She smiled and said, "I can't judge you for what you do, as long as you keep what you do away from me. Just don't bring the problems and we are all good."

He chuckled and said to her, "Well, we good then. Where do you see us going if we ever get together?"

She said, "I like you so far. I just want to go slow and see where this will go with us. I am not trying to rush anything and get hurt."

He couldn't believe how the conversation with her just flowed. He was willing to put it all on the line and be the man she wanted him to be. She also herself maybe our stay just the man I need in my life. Right now, she didn't have any complaints from him, but only time would tell if love conquered all.

She drifted off to sleep. She had no idea where he was taking her. All she knew was they were going to be gone all week, and this was what she needed: a much-needed vacation. She was going to go with the flow and let him spoil her if that was what he wanted to do.

He enjoyed the flight while she slept. He caught up on some much-needed work for some of his businesses. He was also looking into buying another building to possibly open a boutique and thought maybe they could go into business together. He wanted to make sure he could help her build a brand nobody could compare to. He thought he could see himself spending the rest of his life with her just from their conversation. He knew that was some crazy shit, and it even shocked him because they had just met today. He was going to do his best to be the best nigga he could be to her. He would hate to hurt her pretty little soul.

Chapter Four

Falling in love/ the getaway

When she woke up, she noticed they had just arrived in Las Vegas. She hadn't been to Vegas in years, and what better way to spend it than with someone so damn fine and handsome. She smiled at him, and he chuckled back.

"You finally awake, sleepy head. You slept the entire way here."

"Yes, I must have been tired because I was out. I'm sorry I left you up."

He chuckled and told her, "Oh, no problem, get your beauty rest because we are about to have a ball this week. I always come to Vegas when I want to chill out, get away from Detroit and gamble a little."

She told him, "Oh, I don't mind, it's been years since I've been here. I am so happy you decided to bring me here."

Getting off the jet, there was already a car waiting for them. When Miracle asked Iman if they were getting a rental, he simply told her they didn't need a car because they were going to explore Vegas together, walk and have a ball.

We checked into the MGM casino right on the strip, which was an excellent idea. Iman had the car waiting for us so we could do some shopping for our trip and have clothes. First, I needed to check in with Sasha and see how the store was going while Iman checked on his business.

She called Sasha, and Sasha answered, happy to hear from her BFF.

Sasha said, "Hey, boo, how is your trip going?"

"Well, BFF, my trip is going well. We just got here and got off the jet. He is such a gentleman. We talked and had a good flight."

"Where are you guys staying while you're there?"

"We are staying at MGM in Vegas, but heffa, I know damn well you knew who Iman was when I was telling you about him."

Sasha told Miracle, "Yes, I know who Iman is, I just want you to be happy. I am actually dating his friend, Brian."

"So, that's how Iman got all my information. Well, I thank you for looking out for me. I was just calling to check in on business before we go shopping, and to tell you I was here, I love you and to make sure you go to my house and check on it. I got to go, it looks like he is ready to hit the town."

"OK, boo. Have a good trip, enjoy yourself and don't call me again. I will call you if something goes wrong, which we know it won't. Goodbye."

Iman walked into the living room in the suite we were sharing.

"Are you ready to go?"

"Yes, I am. Iman, why didn't you tell me your friend was dating my friend?"

"Well, because I wanted to show you I am not like any of those other niggas. I am true to my word and true to this relationship if you are willing to give me a chance."

She smiled so hard. "Iman, let's just see how this day ends before we become committed to each other because I am not up for games and being played and getting my heart broken. I mean, so far, you have shown me you are a man of your word, and you really have me smiling so we will see."

He and I walked out of the room holding hands and making small talk as we got into the car that was waiting for them to go shopping.

He told her they were going to the Las Vegas North Premium Outlets because they had a lot of stores and he was sure she would like to shop in them.

"You don't have to spend any of your money."

She wanted to get him a gift for taking her on this trip and to show her appreciation.

The first store they hit was Foot Locker because they both knew they would need some gym shoes to do all the walking he was talking about. They looked around and decided on some of the same shoes. They both got a pair of all white Forces and some Air Max. She also saw two pairs of Pumas she just needed to add to her closet. He got a few pair of basketball shorts to lounge in and some t-shirts. He paid for the items and left that store.

They hit Lady Foot Locker, and he paid for her items. They also decided to hit the Burberry store. They got matching shirts, sneakers, and she got two swimsuits. He also got some swim trunks.

"Let's meet back at Foot Locker in an hour." She wanted to get a few things.

He agreed and gave her his black card, and we went on our way.

She went into Victoria's Secret to get some panties, bras and something sexy to wear for him, but she wasn't saying he was going to get some pussy on the first night. She also got a few body sprays, lotions, and soaps for their stay. She went into a few more stores and got something for going out. She got a few more fits and sandals for the stay as well. She wanted to make sure she got him something nice. She hadn't shopped for a man in so long. She went overboard with her own black card. She ended up getting him a few more fits, some Converse, and a few smell goods. She also got them some candles and ended up purchasing him some diamond studs and a Cartier watch.

He didn't spare any expenses when shopping for her. He wanted her to know he was serious about her. He had gotten her a heart-shaped chain, diamond studs, a few purses, some other fits, and shoes. He didn't have a problem spending money on someone who was worth it. While he was shopping, he received a text alerting him that she was ready and waiting for him at Foot Locker. Tonight, he was going to take her out to eat and maybe a little dancing. If she thought this trip was something, just wait to see what he did for her on Valentine's Day. He was going to go all out.

Walking through the outlet, they both had their minds in other places. They couldn't believe how real this felt. It had been so long for both of them, they didn't want to fail at a relationship. When he got to Foot Locker, he laughed. He couldn't believe how many damn bags she had. He knew she had to have put a dent in his card. Miracle smiled at Iman when she saw him.

"Hey, there, sir. I see you did some more shopping."

"Hell, it looks like you did a lot of shopping. You had to have put a dent in my card."

"No, I used some of my own money," she laughed. "I didn't want to go overboard with your card because they would've been calling you, so I saved you this time." He couldn't do anything but laugh and take her bags so they could go.

"So, what's next?"

"Well, I think we should go back to our suite, get out of these hot-ass Detroit clothes, shower and relax. Then we can go to dinner, and maybe dancing. Are you down?"

"Hell yeah, I'm down. Let's go, my king."

He paused, chuckled and kissed Miracle for the first time, and her lips were so fucking sweet, and her breath tasted sweet. He could only imagine what her pussy was hitting on. Her panties instantly got wet, and she couldn't believe he had just kissed her. She knew right then it was going to be hard to contain herself and keep her goods to herself while on this trip.

Once they were outside in the hot-ass Vegas weather, he loaded the car with their items. She got into the car and waited for him. He got in the car and started making small talk with her while they were on their way back to the hotel. When they arrived at the hotel, the bellhop helped them with their bags and took the items to their room. Once they arrived at their room, they put all their things away. She noticed there were a few bags not put away and he noticed the same thing. She wanted to go ahead and give him his gifts.

"Do you want a drink?"

"Yeah, you know what I like."

He prepared their drinks, and he came back into the bedroom. She had laid his items on the bed for him and had a little speech ready and everything. She didn't know what he would think once she said what she had to say, all she knew was that he made her feel comfortable and she was ready to be in a relationship. He didn't know what to think, but her facial expression told it all.

"I know I just met you, but I feel like I am falling in love with you. I was rude when we first met, and I am so sorry, but you have proved to be a stand-up guy. I appreciate you taking me on this trip, so I purchased you a few items to show my appreciation."

He put their drinks down and looked at the items. "Damn, shorty, you didn't have to buy me anything. Everything I did for you was out the kindness of my heart and because I am actually feeling you. One day, I want to make you my wife. I know it's early, but just give me a shot."

He was happy, and it showed. No woman had ever bought him anything, not even Janay. That showed just how much she was really feeling him. She had bought him diamond studs, a Cartier watch, a few pair of shoes and clothes.

"Thank you. I appreciate everything. You are the first woman to buy me anything. I actually got you a few items as well."

When he gave her the items, she couldn't believe he had bought her all of those things. He had bought purses, shoes, and jewelry. She couldn't control herself, so she kissed him. They put the rest of the things away and sipped their drinks. Before they knew it, they had drunk the whole damn bottle of Patrón.

She told him while he was lying down, "I'm about to go get in the shower."

"OK, baby, go ahead. I will use the shower out here in the living area."

While in the shower, she plugged up her phone and let the sweet sounds of Tamar take her to another place. She was in her own world. She got out the shower, wrapped a towel around her and entered the room. He was still in the shower, so she dried off and started putting on her lotion and body spray. She decided on a white bodycon dress that was see-through with a white lace bra and panty set. She also chose to wear strappy white Louboutins. She sprayed her perfume and put on her diamond studs and chain that he had bought her and let her hair stay curly.

She looked in the mirror, and she looked damn good. He walked into the room, cheesing. He thought she looked so fucking good in that dress. He, too, had decided on all-white linen shorts, a white Gucci shirt, and white Gucci loafers. He couldn't let the night go by without telling her how good she looked.

"Damn, you look good. Do you want to skip out on dinner and dancing?"

"No, sir, let's go. I am already drunk, and I am ready to eat and party," she said with a laugh.

They decided on The Palm restaurant and were also going to club 837 to party. Neither of them had been there but had heard they had the best food and that the club was the hottest club there. He just wanted her to have a good time while on his watch.

Chapter Five

Dinner and drinks

Once they arrived at the restaurant, the hostess took them to a private area where they would be having dinner. In that moment, she felt she was in love with him. When they conversed, he talked a good game, saying this was what he wanted, she just didn't want to get hurt in the process. Tonight, however, she wanted to lay it all out on the table. She just wondered what things would be like once they made it back to Detroit.

"Oh my God, this is so beautiful. Thank you."

"No problem, baby girl. Anything to see you smile. Here, let me pull your chair out for you."

"Thank you."

"Let me get around the table so I can sit and look at your sexy ass. You are killing that dress tonight."

"This is so nice. I am having such a good time. This is going to be a date and trip to remember."

"Baby girl, there will be more dates and trips for you to remember. I plan to make it all about you at all times."

The waiter arrived with a bottle of sweet red wine and told them their food would be out soon. She looked at him because they hadn't ordered anything.

"Don't worry, baby. I already ordered our dinner. We'll have a bit of everything from seafood to steak. I really want us to enjoy the meal and this time away from the real world."

"What is your full name?"

"Iman Juan Harris. What is your full name?"

"Mine is Miracle Lanay Captains."

"Yeah, soon to be Mrs. Harris," he chuckled.

"Oh, is that so, Mr. Harris?"

"When I say something, I mean exactly what I said."

"Well, I'm going to lay it all out on the table then," she said. "From where I'm sitting, I can tell we're both feeling each other, and honestly, I'm starting to fall in love with you. Even though it's early, I can't help how I feel, but I want to know where this is going."

"I appreciate you being honest with me about your feelings. Honestly, I haven't felt this way in a long time. Since my ex. I won't say I'm in love with you, but I definitely love you. I'm willing to give you my all in exchange for loyalty, respect, and not making me look like a fool in these streets."

She smiled and reached across the table to kiss her man. She couldn't have been happier to say that he, the King of Detroit, was her man.

He told her he couldn't wait to get her back to the room to make sweet, passionate love to her and show her how a woman should be treated. Right when those words escaped his mouth, the food arrived. The waiter set up all kinds of food and desserts. She had almost told him, *fuck this food, let's go back to the room now and get started.*

She looked at all the food and said, "Who do you think is going eat all of this food? It sure won't be me."

"Well, baby, just eat what you can. We about to have a ball tonight and let Vegas know that Detroit is in the house."

They ate and made small talk, getting to know each other more, telling each other about their goals, dreams and where they planned to be in five years. They also talked about her expanding her business and opening another location. She thought it was crazy that he was all about seeing her achieve her goals. He wanted to invest in her business and see how they could become business partners, which didn't sound like a bad idea at all. Once they were done eating, he paid the tab, and they walked two doors down where the club was located. Vegas, at this time of the year, was so lit. They could hear the music from outside, and whoever the DJ was, he was really kicking out some fire. She was ready to dance, she just hoped he could keep up.

"Are you ready, pretty lady?"

"Yeah, let's get in here and show them how we do it."

Walking right by the security guard and going into the building, they went straight to VIP. There were a few celebrities in the building as well. They had two bottles of Patrón and some Moët on the table. The club was lit, and everyone was dancing. They sat in the area and enjoyed the drinks. They made small talk, and he sat back and chilled, and she danced in her spot. She looked like she was ready to get out on the floor. He wasn't really a dancer, but for her, he would get on the floor.

"Are you enjoying yourself?"

"Yes, baby, let's dance."

She got up to dance to the song that was on, which was, "Wild Thoughts". She was having all kinds of wild thoughts, dancing and swaying her hips on him. He was so in the zone, the liquor had him lit. He didn't mind dancing with her, but if she kept on, the night was going to end right here. He pulled her close to him and sang in her ear. She could feel his thick-ass dick, and she couldn't wait to ride his dick tonight.

He started kissing her neck and said, "Baby, let's take our drunk asses back to the room." She couldn't do anything but follow his lead because she was super lit. They were so lit, they hardly made it out the club. When they got back to the hotel and got into the elevator, she couldn't keep her hands off him. She was trying to pull his dick out his pants and let him have it right there.

He was breathing so hard, saying, "Wait, wait, wait, baby, we about to get off. You know they got cameras."

"I don't care about no damn cameras."

When those words escaped her mouth, the ding of the elevator sounded, and they were in their suite. They started yanking each other's clothes off, kissing and sucking on each other. He picked her up and had her against the wall, sucking the hell out of her pussy. She was having orgasm after orgasm. She hoped she hadn't bitten off too much.

Once he put her down, she got on her knees and put all ten inches of his dick in her mouth. She swirled her tongue around the shaft of his dick, relaxed her throat and started deep throating all ten inches. She could have sworn she heard his toes crack because she was just that good. Before he could stop her, his knees started to buckle, and all his kids went right down her throat. She swallowed every bit of his nut.

He picked her up, laid her on the bed and kissed all over her body. He entered her, and she felt all ten inches in her stomach. This man pounded her shit like it was the last pussy on earth. Moaning and screaming were all that could be heard in the room. He flipped her over and went to work from the back. She came repeatedly, and he thought he had gotten the best of her, but he hadn't. She got on top of him and rode the fuck out of his dick. She had him screaming her name, and when he came, he looked like he was ready to put his thumb in his mouth and go to sleep.

"Come and get in the shower."

Once they got into the shower, they went at it again and again. Once they decided to get out, which was an hour later, they were both wrinkled as hell. They washed up, dried off and got in bed.

"I love you."

"I love you, too."

Chapter Six

Near the ending

He woke up before her on the last day of their trip. They had done so much on this trip. He thought about how much they had learned about each other. They ate, they danced, they shopped, and the most important thing was they had learned more about each other and had become a couple. He hoped that bitch Janay really stayed the fuck away from him, and most importantly, her. He would hate to have to hurt that silly bitch because she couldn't understand that when he said he was done, he meant it. He took it upon himself to go ahead and pack all their things, making sure they didn't leave anything behind. He also went out to the mall to get something comfortable for them to wear on their flight back to Detroit. It was the beginning of January, and it was below zero in Detroit.

He also ordered them breakfast. He wanted them to spend a little more time with each other before they took off. He decided to jump in the shower so that by the time he got out, he could wake her up so she could get herself together as well. Walking into the bathroom, he took his usual morning shit, washed his face, brushed his teeth and prepared his water so that the temperature was just right. While he did that, he decided to run a bubble bath for her so he could wake her up when he was done. He jumped in the shower, and the water relaxed his muscles. It felt so good, he almost didn't want to get out the shower. He washed his body and thought about how he didn't want to leave Vegas. He thought about how he could stay here forever. He knew he needed to get back home to take care of business. So far, everything had been running smoothly. Even with his team expanding, everything was running smoothly.

Stepping out the shower, he didn't expect her to be standing there looking so damn good. He wrapped his towel around his waist.

"Good morning, baby."

"Good morning, bae. Why didn't you wake me up so I could pack?"

"I didn't want to wake you, and I already packed all of our things. I also ran you a bath as well so you can relax while I set up breakfast."

"You didn't have to do that. I could have packed our things."

"I know you could have, but you were sleeping, so I decided to let you sleep. Baby, go ahead and take your bath. Your clothes are out on the bed. I went out to the mall earlier to get a few items for our flight home since all we had was summer clothing."

"OK, thank you. Come give me a kiss."

He walked over to her and kissed her sweet lips. Even though she had just woken up and hadn't brushed her teeth yet, they were still sweet. He knew he loved her, everything about her, even her stank breath and all. She couldn't believe he had actually gotten up early and gone shopping for their trip back home so they could be prepared for the weather. He also took the time to order breakfast, pack all their belongings and run her a bubble bath. This trip was exactly what she needed, and she hated to leave, but she had a business to run, so she needed to get home. Plus, she missed her BFF Sasha.

Relaxing in this tub was wonderful. He had done everything just right, she just hoped once they get home, they could stay close and make this relationship work since they were both busy running businesses. She got out the bathtub, dried off, and brushed her teeth before going into the room with her towel wrapped around her body. She found her outfit sitting on the bed: a pair of blue, distressed jeans, a white fitted shirt, a nice pair of panties and bra, and blue UGGs with UGG warmers. She got dressed and went to find her man sitting at the table, putting the finishing touches on breakfast. When she spotted him, she smiled.

"Well, hello, how was your bath?"

"It was wonderful. Thank you so much for everything."

"No need to thank me. You look nice and ready to go back home."

"I wish we could stay a little longer."

"I feel the same way."

His phone started ringing, and he looked at it. He excused himself, but she could hear him in the room yelling, "Why do you keep fucking calling me, Janay?"

"I already explained to you that we're fucking done. I don't want shit to do with you so stop fucking calling me. I have a woman, and she won't like you calling me."

She shook her head. From the looks of it, his ex couldn't get enough of his ass. *She better stay in her place because I don't mind putting a bitch on her ass about mine.* He walked back in the kitchen with a heated expression on his face. She didn't want to say anything to him because she didn't know how he would respond.

"My bad, I had to take that call and set my ex straight," he told her because he knew she had heard his call. "She can't seem to let go or understand that I don't want anything to do with her."

"Oh, you good, baby. As long as that bitch don't start any shit, then I won't have to beat her ass. I stay ready and keep a Glock on me at all times so anybody can get it."

"OK, now you gangsta, huh? Girl, what am I going to do with your ass? Come on, let's eat so we can get up out of here."

"I don't know what I'm going to do with you."

"I already know what you working with between your legs. That monster got your ex-girl going."

He chuckled so hard, he started choking on his orange juice. "Girl, please eat your food. You trying to kill me already.

"No, I was just telling the truth, daddy."

Chapter Seven

Detroit / Sasha and B

She was happy because she had been taking care of everything while her BFF was gone out of town with him. The boutique was doing so well, and she couldn't have been happier about going into business with her best friend. They had been friends since elementary school, and she had been more of a sister than a friend to her. They had each other's back.

When Miracle told Sasha about the guy she had met at the Starbucks, she didn't know it was her man, Brian's best friend, Iman. Everyone knew who Iman and Brian were in the streets, but Miracle was so busy with the boutique, she wasn't really out there like that. Especially since that lame-ass nigga Cameron had fucked her over about six months ago. She had never seen her girl so hurt before in her life. She and Cam had been together since high school, and she never thought that nigga would do her so dirty, but what was done in the dark would come to light.

People had always tried to warn her about his ass, but she was too in love with his dirty ass. When my man Brian called me and told me about Iman meeting someone, he didn't have to go any further because I already knew who he was talking about. I gave him my girl's info and told my man to make sure he hooked Iman and Miracle up. I was tired of Miracle walking around, not having a life at all. It was time for her to get her shit together.

Brian and I had been dating for a few months. Don't get me wrong, dating a nigga who was into hustling wasn't all bad. What kind of fucked me up were the bitches who didn't have any respect when they knew he was taken. I hadn't had any issues with any females over Brian yet, but I knew everything wouldn't stay peachy.

Brian and I got along very well. He said he loved my go-getter attitude, and he loved the fact that I didn't nag him about his well-being and what he was doing when we were not together, which was true. I had a business to run, so we talked when we talked. I mean, don't get me wrong, we started our mornings off with a good morning text and ended our nights with a goodnight text.

I had met Brian one day in the mall when I was shopping for a gift for my parents' anniversary. He said he was with his boy, but I never saw this "boy". I knew who Brian was because everyone knew everyone in Detroit. We exchanged numbers, and ever since then, we had been kicking it, going out on dates. We spent nights with each other when we could get some time away from our businesses.

I kept Brian a secret until I knew whether this was short term or long term. I told Brian to make sure he kept his business away from me. I never wanted to be caught up in the bullshit. Enough things were going on in Detroit, and I didn't want to end up on the news for being killed. Brian knew as long as he respected my wishes, he could have this pussy whenever he wanted it.

I truly couldn't wait until my girl comes back from Vegas. I hadn't talked to her while she was there except for one time, which was when they first touched down. Everything must have been going well because she hadn't called me or flown her ass back to Detroit. I knew they were scheduled to come home today, so I wanted her to come into the store and have very little to do. I swear my girl needed to loosen up some and have some fun.

I swear I hoped she gave that nigga some ass because she needed some dick in her life, for real. I had been texting Brian all day off and on, and he wanted to go out to dinner tonight. He even said maybe we could double date with Iman and Miracle.

I told him that would be a good idea and I would keep him posted on what was going on because you could never be sure about Miracle's attitude sometimes.

Brian could be so up and down sometimes. I could honestly see him opening up more soon because our feelings for each other were getting deep. I just prayed that everything worked out for us and nothing came between us because what he didn't know was that I would drop his ass like a bad habit and he wouldn't know what hit his ass. I didn't take any bullshit. I didn't care who you were and what kind of money you made, you would not make a fool of me. I was a boss, making things happen, and didn't need a nigga for shit, so we would see.

I needed to go out here and put out all the new inventory. There were so many things that had come in from last week's order for the store. We had to be different. There were a lot of boutiques in Detroit, but none like The Eternity Look Boutique. I knew my girl would be home soon and walk through those doors, trying to find something wrong, so I was going to make sure everything and everyone were on point.

Chapter Eight

Back home

Our flight was so nice getting back home. Arriving at the airport, I had B come get my car and bring my truck and leave it. We had so many damn bags, and I wanted her to be comfortable on her ride back home.

"Baby, where is your car?"

"B came and got it and brought my truck since you had so many bags."

"Oh, no, don't blame it on me. You love shopping as much as I do. You have just as many bags as I do."

Once he got all the bags in the truck, he made sure to help her in the truck.

"Let me stop by my house so I can put my things up, then I'll take you home. I know you have to go to work, so I am going to drop you off and come back and get you when you get off."

"You don't have to do all that. I can drive myself."

"It's no big deal. Plus, my boy texted me and said he wanted to have dinner with us.

"I'll let you know once I get to the store and see how the day goes. We've been gone all week and I kinda just want to chill tonight."

"Well, let me know. Either way, I am going to be with you tonight."

"Yes, it's cool, baby."

Pulling up to his house, it was so nice on the outside. She didn't know he lived so close to her. No wonder it hadn't taken him long to get to her house the other night. He pulled into his driveway, put his code in and pulled up in front of his door. He had all kinds of cars outside. No wonder when I tried to give him his black card back he told me to keep it, and that he was going to add me to his account. She was shocked, to say the least, but he must have been feeling her. She was in the zone and hadn't heard him calling her.

"Oh, my bad, I was in my own world."

"Oh OK, come on and come in for a minute. Let me put this stuff in the house."

I got out the truck, and when he opened the door and let me in, his house was very nice, and it was decorated so nicely.

"Who decorated?"

He paused then said, "Well, I'm going to be honest. Me and my ex used to live together, so she decorated."

He walked away, going up the stairs, telling me to make myself at home and that he would be back down in a minute. Looking around his house, the kitchen was to die for. His whole house was nice, really. He didn't have many pictures up, but a few of him and his boys, some of which she recognized from around the way. She wondered why they had never crossed paths before. She knew had they encountered one another, she would have remembered him. He came back downstairs and didn't see me until he found me in his theater room.

"Do you like the house?"

"Yes, it is very nice and very well decorated."

"Thank you. Maybe one day you can decorate and change some things for me if you wouldn't mind."

I smiled at him. "We need to go. I need to get to work."

He told me he had to change and grab some money, and he needed to check on his businesses.

"Did you think about what we talked about in Vegas?" he asked.

"Yes, let me talk with Sasha, and I'll get back to you about it."

"OK. In the meantime, I'll try to line up some buildings so we can check them out."

He walked over and kissed her on the lips. He locked the house up after setting the alarm, and they were back on the road. He pulled up to her house, and she told him he could come on in and make himself at home. She went up to her room while he carried the rest of her bags to her room. She was in her walk-in closet, getting something else to put on. It didn't matter what the weather was, she dressed to kill on a daily, so today would be no different. She found a high waisted skirt with a cute, sheer blouse, and boots that stopped right at her knee. She grabbed a thong, a bra, and some fishnets. Walking out of the closet, she saw him laid back on her bed, looking like a whole snack, watching TV.

She started undressing, and he wasn't paying her any attention. He must have been in his own world. Once she was done dressing, she changed purses and decided to carry her black Hermes purse since she had the belt on. She grabbed her waist-length mink jacket and told him she was ready. He finally looked up, and he looked like he'd seen a model. He couldn't believe she was going to work looking like that, but on second thought, yes he could. She was just that fly. It was cold outside, and her hair was up in a tight bun, so she had her mink headband on as well. She looked in the mirror and knew she was that bitch. She thought he was silly as hell, and he kept her laughing. He must not know he had a diva on his hands. She was a bad bitch at all times; there wasn't any slacking.

He pulled up to her place of business, which was in the heart of Downtown Detroit. She gave him a kiss on the lips before getting out the truck and told him she would text him about tonight and let him know what time to pick her up if she wanted to go to dinner tonight.

"OK."

He got out and opened the door for her. As soon as he closed the door and gave her a hug, some bitch came up. Janay walked up to his truck after seeing him hugging some bitch.

"So, this is why you can't give us another chance?"

He turned around, and I could see the veins in his forehead. He was pissed off. I just stood there to see how he was going to handle this situation, especially with it being in front of my store.

He started yelling, "Janay, why the fuck are you here?"

She looked at him and said, "No, Iman, answer my question! Is this bitch the reason you can't fuck with me no more?"

Before you know it, I turned my head and looked down the street because I knew damn well this bitch wasn't talking about me.

"Listen, honey, I am not going to be too many more of your bitches, so I'm going to need you to pipe down before there's a problem."

Janay laughed and said, "Bitch, pipe down, this is not what you want. I was talking to him, not your bougie ass."

He told me, "Baby, I got this." Iman looked pissed off.

"Look, Janay, we are over and done. I don't want you, and I told you that shit last week. We've been broken up for months, just leave me the fuck alone."

I looked at him and whoever this bitch was and told him, "I don't have time for this shit, let me get to work. I'll text you later about what we talked about, but take care of this trash. I can't have this outside my business." Iman kissed me, and all hell broke loose. This bitch tried to grab my hair, but before she could grab at me, I had my .40 pointed dead at her face.

"Bitch, if you don't get the fuck back, I promise on everything I love, you won't make it home. I'll send your ass straight to your maker. Now make me act a fool."

"Bitch, you got me this time, but I'm going to see you again. Let's see if you tough then."

He pushed the bitch so hard, she fell. He yelled, "Get the fuck on, Janay, before you come up missing!"

She was crying so hard, she got up and walked away.

By now, Sasha had come outside and was yelling, "Do we have a problem?"

"Take your crazy ass back inside. Here I come."

"OK."

I told Iman, "Look, you need to get rid of her. She is going to be a fucking problem. I can't have anybody coming by my business, setting it on fire or any other bullshit. Handle that bitch before I do, OK?"

He looked like, *who the hell is this woman, and where is my Miracle?* Iman told me, "Baby, I got this. I am about to handle this, OK? Give me some love. Have a good day, and I'll see you later." He gave me a kiss, and I went into the building.

Walking into the building, I spoke. "Good afternoon, everyone."

"Hey, Ms. Miracle."

I told Sasha to meet me in the back. I stopped and said, "Oh, the store looks nice, you guys, keep up the good work."

Going into our office, I put my coat and bag up but made sure I kept my gun on my desk because you never knew what you might have to do.

Sasha came into the office. "So, what the fuck was that all about, sis?"

"Man, Sash, that was Iman's old bitch. She had been calling him the whole time we were out of town, and he told her ass he didn't want anything to do with her. He told me she cheated on him."

"Yeah, she might have been at the nail salon next door when she saw you guys."

"Yeah, I bet she learned her lesson today. Don't try to grab me if you don't want a full clip in your ass."

Sasha cracked up laughing. "How was your trip, Miracle?"

"I had a ball. We shopped, we ate, we danced, we walked around, we got drunk, and we fucked like crazy, girl. Iman is something else."

Sasha said, "I am so glad you like him, girl. Now you can come out your funk and join me and B."

"Yes. So, he told me you're dating his best friend, which leads to my next question. You told me you were dating someone, but you know, you never really bring him around, and you never gave an answer why."

Sasha said, "Well, it's not like that, it's just that I wanted to keep him a secret until I knew exactly what was going on with us. You know how niggas are, so I didn't want to jinx anything."

"It's cool, girl, but are you happy?"

"I'm happy. That man is everything and then some to me."

"Well, as long as I don't have to pop his ass."

"Oh my God, Miracle, you stay wanting to shoot someone."

Sasha asked, "So, what's going on with you and Iman?"

"Well, as you can see, he is my man now. Everything was going well until this little trick-ass bitch showed up, making me act an ass."

"Yes, Miracle has a man! I hope he can handle your ass because he just doesn't know you're something else."

"We going out to eat tonight, or are you and Iman going out?"

"He was saying something to me about it, but I told him I needed to see what was going on in the store. I think I'm going to let him know that we can go ahead and go out. I need to meet this guy you're talking about."

Things at work had been going great. Everything was done, and I had been in the office all day, going over the books, ordering new inventory and getting some things in for the spring. I could put them in the back for when the season changed. I loved to be on top of things and made sure we didn't get too behind on anything in the fashion world. I hadn't heard from Iman, so I decided to text him.

Me: Hey, baby, did you handle that problem? How is your day going?

My Baby: Hey, baby, I am a little busy right now, but my day is going OK. Let me text you back and make sure you let me know what time to get you. Love you, bye.

Me: I love you, too, and OK. Be here about 6:30.

My Baby: OK, baby.

I read my text; that was a little weird. Oh well, let me finish doing what I am doing. I can't let that get to me. I will see him later on today.

On the other side of town, Iman and Janay were going at it. Janay couldn't get it in her mind that they were done, over, never going to be an item again in life.

"So, you just moved on so fucking quick like me, and you weren't about to get married?"

"I don't give a fuck about none of that. If you had kept the next nigga's dick out your mouth, we would still be together, but since you couldn't, bitch, I am done with you. I've been done with your dumb ass, but you couldn't leave well enough alone."

Janay looked at Iman like he was crazy. "I am never leaving you alone. I love you, and I want my man back. You can get rid of that bougie-ass bitch because nobody can take care you like I can. So, get it done or I'm going to the police about your whole fucking operation."

He cracked his neck because he couldn't believe the same woman he had taken care of had threatened him. Before she could get another word out her mouth, he had his hands wrapped around her neck.

"Bitch, you just can't keep your fucking mouth shut. You just have to keep fucking up. If I say I'm done with your ass, Janay, leave it at that and finish being a jump off, fucking that nigga you cheated on me with. I don't have time for your petty-ass bullshit."

He dropped the bitch on the ground. He knew letting her live would be his biggest mistake. She laughed; something was truly wrong with her. She had some screws loose, and he couldn't understand why she couldn't just leave him alone.

"Do you think you scared me? You taught me not to fear shit. I've been with your ass so long, I know your whole operation. Hell, we're in the warehouse where you store most of your shit anyway."

She kept going, feeling herself because she thought he would never hurt her. She thought if she threatened him, he would leave the bitch alone. He cared so much about his operation, but she was about to find out that not only did he care about his operation, he also cared about his woman. He used to feel the same way about her until she did him wrong. Now he couldn't stand her ass. He sent a text to B to let him know he was in the warehouse and to get the cleanup crew there asap because he needed them. He knew then he needed to kill that bitch. She had done the number one thing he'd told her not to do, which was threaten his operation. He stood up, went to fix himself a shot of Patrón and threw the shot back. He pulled his gun out and blew her brains out. She would never know what hit her dumb ass. If she thought she was going to keep threatening his empire, this bitch was crazy. She thought she was going to talk about Miracle like she was crazy, then the bitch had another thing coming. Poof be gone. The bitch had to disappear, and forever, he just hoped this didn't come back to bite him in the ass.

I sat back down to wait for the cleanup crew to come and took more shots. The fact that I had to kill my ex-fiancée had me fucked up. He knew it was either him or her, and he'd be damned if it would be him. He wasn't going down because she couldn't let go of the dick. He would always love her, but he had a new woman, and nobody was ever going to change that. B and two of their workers, Lil John and Stevie, walked into the warehouse. B looked at Janay and back at him and couldn't believe he had really shot her ass.

"What the fuck, nigga? That's Janay."

"Yeah, I know who the fuck it is. I bet you next time that bitch will think before she speaks."

B just shook his head and told them to get rid of her body and burn her car as well.

He went into his office with the bottle and B followed him.

"Mani, what the fuck happened?"

"This bitch ran up on Miracle and me while I was dropping her off at her store this afternoon. Janay was talking crazy as hell, so Miracle had to pull out on her ass."

B shook his head. He had no idea all this had gone down today. He knew his boy killing her ass was going to fuck with him. He knew his boy must really be feeling this girl because he had shot his ex and was going all out for her. He had his boy's back if nobody else didn't have his back. Even though she was sis, you never go against the grain, no matter what the situation was. You had to learn to take the punches on the chin and roll with them at all cost. He didn't want to know any more details about what had happened today. Everything was taken care of, so as long as the threat was eliminated, that was all that mattered. My boy was just sitting there looking lost. I know it hurt, but oh well, our life must go on.

He said, "Well, nigga, it's almost time for me to pick her up from work. I'll hit you up and let you know what's up with dinner tonight, depending on how she feels after this afternoon."

He stood up, gave his boy a handshake and left the office. The guys had taken care of everything, and it smelled like bleach. When he got outside, even the bitch's car was gone. He got in his truck and went to pick up his lady. He had missed her. She saw the time was six PM. She couldn't wait to get off her feet, they were killing her. Sasha and the other workers had already left for the day because they were kind of slow. On Mondays, they usually just did inventory. She wanted to finish pricing some items. She heard the bell ring, and in came one of the sexiest men she had ever seen.

She went to get her gun from under the counter. She'd had it there since she was the only one in the store at the time. She didn't want to be caught slipping, being alone, and be an easy target. She went to the back where her office was so she could cut off her computer, turn off the lights and check the back door. He must have followed her into the office. He sat down while she got the rest of her items. His mind was all over the place, and he was just ready to chill and get a drink.

He opened the door to the truck for her, and when she sat down, it felt so good. It was so cold outside. She could smell the liquor on his breath. She hadn't even asked him why he had been drinking early in the day. He looked like he'd had a bad day. Her feet were hurting, and she was ready to change. This had been a bad day. She should have taken today off as well. Coming in from a flight and going straight to work was not a good idea. The whole ride was quiet, so she put her head back to relax and rest her eyes until he got to her house. Looking over at her, she was knocked out. He thought about sending a text to B to suggest having a sleepover at his house, and he would cook dinner. He just wanted to relax, and since she was already sleeping, he thought that was the best thing to do.

Me: My lady a little tired. Why don't you and Sis pack an overnight bag and come to the house and we cook dinner and chill tonight? Maybe we can go out over the weekend.

My Brother: Shit, Sasha said that's cool. I'll be to your house around eight. Anything you need at the store?

Me: Tell Sasha to get whatever it is her and my lady like to eat, and you get some shit for us.

My Brother: OK, I'll see you later.

He didn't even respond. We pulled up to her house, and he woke her up. When she got up, she couldn't believe she had slept so long. She must have been tired. Today was an eventful day for both of them. She got out the truck, and so did he, right behind her.

"What time is dinner?"

"Well, there's been a change of plans. Sasha and B are coming over to my house, so I'm going to cook dinner for them."

She sent out a text to Sasha to tell her to text the workers to let them know they could have the day off. She knew she needed a day off, and she also knew Sasha needed one as well because she had been working all week in the store while they were in Vegas.

He got out to open the door for her, helping her out the truck. She went to open her door and disarmed her alarm. They went into the house, and she went upstairs to her room to change her clothes. He sat on the couch, and her doorbell rang.

"You expecting company?"

"No. How, when we just got here. Just get the door for me, and I'll be right down."

He went to the door and standing there was some black-ass nigga. At first, he was a little taken aback that some guy was standing at her door. He had to collect himself before he went the fuck off. He didn't want to piss her off in the process if nothing was going on between her and dude, but he was going to find out just who he was. He couldn't become a threat to their relationship. The guy stared at this brown-skinned nigga opening her door like he stayed there and paid bills there.

"Aye, who are you, my nigga? Is Miracle home?"

"Me? I'm her man. May we help you? She's a little busy."

"If you don't get your bitch ass the fuck on, I know something."

"She doesn't have a man. Plus, she's batshit crazy."

"Aye, Miracle, where you at?" He had to pinch the top of his nose as he always did when he was mad as hell.

The dude walked past him and came into her house like he was the owner. He didn't want to fuck up her crib, but this nigga was fooling, and he needed to find out who he was. She came downstairs, happy as hell. She didn't think she would see her ex sitting on her couch with her new man standing there. She was dressed to kill with a Bebe jogging suit and UGGs on. She had on her Burberry coat and was ready to leave when she saw who was sitting there. She started yelling once she saw Cameron.

"What the fuck are you doing in my house, nigga? I haven't spoken to you in over six months, and you come to my house like we cool."

"Who is this fuck boy you got in your house?"

"My dog, you got one more time, and I'm going to show you why they call me the King of the D."

"Nigga, mind your business and get the fuck out my house. You already know we not cool and we not happening."

"Don't make me act a fool in here. You already know how I get, and I will shoot your ass again. I don't have any problem letting your ass have it."

He got up and left. One thing he knew was when she was mad, nothing nice would ever come of it. He knew if he didn't leave now, she would shoot him. She had done it before. She was the kind of woman who was scorned and didn't have a problem fucking shit up and leaving. He knew he would see her soon when she least expected it. He wasn't jealous of the nigga she had standing with her. He didn't want her ass back, he was over that bitch. He just knew it was time to go, so he took his chances and left well enough alone.

Iman closed the door. He was pissed the fuck off. Too much was happening in one day and they had just gotten into a relationship. He could only hope in due time things got better. He didn't need anything messing up his operation. He loved her and wanted to be with her, but today must have been ex pop-up day because both of their exes had made a visit today. They must have been able to sense when we were happy, and here they come to destroy some shit.

"I don't know what the fuck he needs, but I will find out today."

"Are you ready to go? I can't take no more today."

She got her purse and told him to lead the fucking way.

"Wait a fucking minute. You got a fucking attitude with me, nigga, your ex-bitch was downstairs."

"I don't have an attitude with you, but this nigga had to call you. How many times does he just pop up?"

"He doesn't ever pop up and hasn't called me because I made sure he was on the blocked list."

He just shook his head and got her bag while she made sure the alarm was on. He got in the truck and was super mad. Now he had beef with a nigga he knew nothing about. He didn't mean to take it out on her, but she must realize he was that nigga in the streets. He didn't even wait for her to get in the truck; he was ready for a drink and ready to lay the fuck down. The whole week had been nice, and today was a good start, but things got in the way once exes came through to fuck shit up and leave. She got in the truck, put her seat belt on and didn't say a word to him. He grabbed her hand, and she pulled away. He didn't pull off because he didn't want them on bad terms.

"I love you, and I am sorry about taking my attitude out on you. Please forgive me."

"It's cool. Can we please just go? I want to lay down."

When he started driving, she took her phone out to send a text message to Erica, who is Cam's sister. She happened to be her other BFF. They had met in ninth grade and had been cool ever since. She and Sasha were the godmother to her daughter, JuJu. Nothing could come between them, not even her punk-ass brother.

Me: Hey, chica.

Sis: Hey, chica. How are you, baby? We need to meet for lunch or dinner, me, you and Sash.

Me: I'm good, baby, and yes, we do. Soon, maybe Sunday. But, question. Cam just popped up here acting a fool once again. Do you know what he wants?

Sis: OK, Sunday is cool. Girl, that fool is not going to learn. Cam talking about you got one of his scales in your basement, and he needs it. I told Cam's dumb ass not to go to your house, leave well enough alone and go buy another one.

Me: E, why couldn't that fool just say that? He comes in here talking crazy cause my bae was here. Talking about he made me and all this other shit. You know I don't have time for his shit, but I will shoot his ass again. How has Mama been?

Sis: Girl, don't I know. Cam's ass is crazy. He only did that shit because he saw you had company. Don't mind him. I will talk to him, and I'll come by tomorrow to pick up the scale, just text me. Girl, Mama is Mama. Still acting a fool, going down to the casino all the time. She trying to get me to go tonight but I told that lady it's cold.

Me: OK, thank you, sis. Just tell Cam to leave me alone. He has his family and the woman he wants. I can move on if I want. Girl, if mama doesn't sit the hell down, it's cold out. I'll text you tomorrow, boo.

Sis: OK, chica, love you.

Me: Love you, too, chica. Kiss my godbaby for me too.

She repeated the text to him, and he couldn't believe this nigga had made a pop-up visit for a scale. See, that was the type of nigga I had no respect for. You come to this woman's house for some shit you could replace. If you were selling weight in the streets, you kept more than one scale anyway. That was how you know who the real weight sellers in the D were, and it wasn't his broke ass. He had some nerve to come to her house, acting a fool over a fucking scale, but I'd see his ass in the streets, don't worry.

She was really thrown off for a minute that Cam had done all that. She knew for a fact he didn't miss her or the relationship because he had made that shit clear when he got his shit and left. He told me he cared for her in the past, but something happened, and he stopped caring about her. He used to always fuck other bitches, and I knew, I just turned a blind eye. She was glad she had met a good nigga, a real man, someone who wouldn't hurt her. She was ready to see his world and be a part of it, even if that meant she had to bust her gun, too. She would do anything for her nigga. They were going to be the new Bonnie and Clyde of the D.

Chapter Nine

Slumber Party

Pulling up to his house, she could see he already had company. It looked like his boy and my girl were already here because we were late as hell. All she thought about on the ride over here was wait until she told Sasha what the hell had just happened. He pulled into his garage and got my bag from the back seat. He unlocked the door, and when we got into the house, the first thing we saw was my girl drinking a glass of wine.

"It took you two long enough."

"Bitch, don't start with me. We got here when we could get here."

He and B just did a head nod since he was the one cooking. Whatever it was he was cooking smelled good, and my stomach started making noise.

"Damn, it smells good in here, homie. You didn't have to cook."

"Nigga, me and mine weren't going to starve and keep waiting for you two slow ass folks to get her."

"You must be the infamous B. Hello, I'm Miracle, Sasha's BFF."

"Oh, I know who you are already, little lady."

"Well, that's nice to know. I'm glad I've been the topic of discussion."

"Sasha, fix me a shot and a glass of wine, please. Let me take my stuff up to his room." Iman and I went up to his room. He hadn't given me a kiss all day, so after he threw my things in his closet, he made sure he kissed my lips. He had been waiting all day to taste her lips. He couldn't keep her lips off his mind. There was something about her that made his day. Even when he was upset, he could think about her and everything would be good. He wished he had a mother so he could take her home to meet her. The way he had grown up, that wasn't even a part of the plan since B's parents had taken him in and taken care of him.

"Damn, baby, I missed you, too."

"Let's not start nothing. We have all night for that. Let's go downstairs."

He said, "Go ahead, baby. Let me get comfortable right quick."

I went downstairs to the kitchen where Sasha and B were. My girl was sitting at the table with my drinks, so I turned the shot up so quick and started sipping my wine. I needed another shot after everything that had transpired today. Words could never explain how angry I really was about this nigga popping up at my house. Sitting back looking at these two, they seemed to really be into each other. As long as Sasha was happy with him, then I was happy for her. She deserved happiness. She took care of everybody but had never had anybody to take care of her. Every nigga she dated was never on any us shit; it was always about them, which left my girl looking stupid in the end. I was just happy she had gotten somebody to make her smile and keep her company when she got lonely.

"Girl, what the fuck wrong with you, taking all these shots like you had a bad day?"

"Girl, why the fuck did Cam come to the house and Iman had to check his ass."

Sasha shook her head. She knew how things could get with Cam and me. She had been there for it all from the beginning to the end. He came into the kitchen with a blunt hanging from his lips. He looked sexy in his basketball shorts and shirt. What a difference being at home made. Earlier, his ass had a big attitude. I wondered what had gone on with him and that bitch.

"Nigga, I just heard what happened. So that's what took so long, huh?"

"Shit has been crazy all day, my nigga. Come to find out, all the nigga wanted was a fucking scale he had left at her house."

B was doubled over laughing so hard. I couldn't believe a nigga had come all the way to someone's house for a fucking scale instead of buying another one. It seemed to me that nigga had another agenda. That was some shit B would never do. That was some bum-ass shit. In his mind, it made him less of a man to show up at his ex's house to cause a scene when you knew you weren't wanted.

"My nigga, you got to be lying. That nigga didn't come over there for a scale."

"She was like please pour me another shot. Hell no, he not lying. Shit was crazy today. We should have stayed in Vegas one more day instead of coming home after dealing with some of this shit we dealt with today."

"So, my nigga, what are you cooking?"

"Steak, shrimp, loaded baked potatoes, a salad, and some broccoli."

"Damn, nigga, you did your thing."

"Yeah, he did do his thing. I'm glad he cooked because I sure didn't feel like it."

"Girl, you weren't about to burn up my fucking stove."

"Come on, Sash, let's set the table. Grab the wine. Oh, and E baby said we need to meet for lunch Sunday afternoon, and I told her OK."

"I miss my sister E. How is our JuJu doing?"

"You know she bad as hell. Maybe we can take her shopping this weekend."

We set the table because the food was almost done. Everything smelled so good, and we had Patrón and wine. Everything seemed to be going well so far. It seemed like Sash was in her zone. She looked like she was thinking about something. If I dug a little later, I was sure she would tell me what had her in the zone. I never noticed how happy she seemed over the past few months. I had been in my own world, making sure our boutique was running smoothly. She was always smiling and singing whenever we were at the store. Now I see what had her so open and happy. They made a good couple. Things were starting to look up for both of us. We both had good men who adored us and cared about us. We knew the devil was always in the back lurking, but we stayed ready for whatever.

Putting the food on our plates, we made small talk with each other. I never knew Sash and B had been dating six months. She had made sure she kept that a secret from me, which was something she never did.

"B, you better treat my BFF right or else you going to have to see me."

He held his hands up. "OK, I got you, sis. I don't want any problems, I hear you gun crazy anyway."

"I know he told you that, but I didn't have a choice. She wasn't going to try to swing on me over some dick."

"Oh, so now I'm just some dick?"

"What I'm saying is, she's going crazy over you and can't get over you. I got the dick, so I know what it is."

"Yeah, OK, as long as you made what you were saying clear."

"Oh, it was clear when I said it the first time."

"OK, you two, please don't act like me and B aren't sitting here, too."

"Baby, they see us. They can't help but see us; we the sexiest couple at the table."

"Sash, let's clear the table, this fool tripping."

Clearing the table and loading the dishwasher, Iman and B smoked a blunt, talking business. I could hear bits and pieces of what they were talking about. One thing about Sash and me, we kept our eyes and ears open. Business must have been going well because they were talking about making an expansion soon or they had already done it. Either way, as long as we didn't get caught up in anything, everything was good. Once the kitchen was cleaned, counters were wiped down, and the food was put away, I knew it was time to change my clothes so I could get comfortable with everyone else.

"Let me go and change my clothes. I shall return."

"OK, girl. Go 'head, I'm about to get these cards and games together."

I gave him a kiss and went upstairs so I could change my clothes. My mind was everywhere with everything that had taken place. Was this God's way of showing me I needed to get out while I could? Or was this God's plan of showing me I deserved to be in love and happy? Really taking in the decorations in his room, everything from the bed to the carpet, curtains, and bath matched. His house was really nice, nicer than mine. I looked at houses in the area, but it was just Cam and me. Well, that was until all the fuck shit happened.

Going into the bathroom, turning on the shower, I saw there was already some soap inside the shower. I'd talk to him about that later. There was no way I would be spending the night at his house, and he still held half of this bitch's belongings here. I was glad I had my own soap and stuff. If he planned on being with me, he was going to have to make sure he got rid of her shit, for real. After taking a shower, I put lotion and body spray on, then I got my Victoria's Secret PINK pajamas out my bag. I had PINK socks as well and house shoes. I was getting ready to go back downstairs when he came into the room. I might as well get this off my chest now because it needed to be taken care of.

"Why do you still have her things here in your house if you two are broken up?"

"What things are you talking about? Nothing in my house belongs to her."

"So, the soap and the clothes aren't hers? Whose are they then?"

"If you don't pipe down. I went shopping earlier and got you a few items for when you're here."

"OK, so all you had to do was tell me that."

"What the fuck do you think I just did? You're tripping for nothing."

"Tripping? I come in here to shower and change clothes, and there's a bitch's soap and clothing here. How do you think I'm supposed to act?"

"You know, I thought we were on the same page, but from this conversation, we're on different paths."

"If you feel like that over a fucking question, I can take my ass to my own house."

"Well, take your ass home then. For one, I won't be putting up with your attitude. If we're going to be together, you're going to have to chill."

"Let me pack my shit, change my clothes and call me an Uber."

"Fuck you, I'm going back downstairs if you change your mind."

"Fuck you, Iman."

I ran into the bathroom and started crying after he went back downstairs. Today had not been my day. Everything was going so well for us, but I knew it was too good to be true. He hadn't given me a reason not to believe him, but he could be telling me anything. When he got back downstairs, he noticed B and Sasha having a conversation, so he walked past them. He needed a shot and another blunt because she had just blown whatever high he had.

"Bro, you OK? Why you look mad?"

"Your girl upstairs tripping about some clothes and soap I brought her. I don't have time for her bull. I told her to take her ass home if she not happy."

"Let me go talk to her. You have to excuse her and her attitude sometimes."

"Yeah, please go talk to her before I throw her ass out in the cold."

"Nigga, you not going to throw her out so shut up."

"OK, you already know how I am, bro. I'll put her ass out quick, fuck love."

"Nigga, come hit this blunt and chill while my baby goes to talk to her."

Walking upstairs, once I got to what I thought was his room, I could hear sniffling and moving around. I hated when she let her attitude get the best of her and ruined everything good she had going. I needed to talk to her because this was the best thing that had happened to her. I just wanted her to be happy and not ruin her happiness. Whatever they were tripping over was stupid. Life was way too fucking short to be arguing over clothing and soaps. Lord, please spare me and let me get up and talk to her crazy ass. She's going to owe me. Hell, they're both going to owe me a shopping spree.

Knock. Knock.

"I don't want to talk to your rude ass. As a matter of fact, I'm taking my ass home."

"Bitch, it is not Iman. It's me, Sash, and I'm coming in, bitch."

"Oh, I'm sorry, sis, come in."

"Bitch, why you in here crying? That man loves the fuck out you. Got his ass down there mad as hell."

"I don't care about him being mad. He could have told me about the clothes and soap before we got here."

"Did you ever think that you both had so much happen today, it wasn't on his mind?"

"No, I didn't because he could have said something when he saw me coming up here earlier, but he didn't say anything at all."

"I am so tired of your ass with these attitudes. That's a down-ass nigga down there."

"I know how down he is, but I won't be hurt again. It's called communication."

"That's fine, but there is a way to communicate. Just don't shut him out. That's all I'm saying."

"I will think about it. What, he sent you up here to talk to me?"

"I know you, so when I saw him upset, I knew I had to talk to you. Come back downstairs and enjoy your night, girl."

"I will think about it."

"OK, mean-ass bitch. Don't make me have to come back up here."

Leaving out his room and shutting the door, I didn't give a fuck that I had gone off and hadn't given her time to speak. I was done being nice to her ass. I was her sister, and I was going to be raw and upfront with her ass, even if it hurt her feelings. I wouldn't be a friend if I couldn't be raw with her and tell her how it was. I had been there with her through it all, so I hurt when she hurt, but I didn't have any problem putting her in her place when she was wrong. Right or wrong, I was standing beside her.

She had always been bougie because we were spoiled, but I blamed Cam for fucking her mind up. Now he had the nerve to show back up. Who does that when they have a whole family and a whole life? I just hoped they could get this together.

Sitting in his room, I took my clothes off and put my pajamas on. I refused to let my attitude fuck up what we had going on. I knew I needed to tone it down some because he wasn't one of those guys who was going to keep taking my bullshit attitude. I still couldn't believe he had told me to get the fuck out his house. He really had some nerve, rude-ass nigga. When I got in the dining room, they were sitting around the table, smoking, and drinking.

"Can I speak to you in private, please?"

"Yeah, let's make this quick. I need another drink."

"I am so sorry about my attitude. I have been through so much in my life, I just don't want to get hurt.

"I love you. Please forgive me."

"I love you, too, but you need to tone it down and let things flow. I told you I won't hurt you."

I went up to him and didn't give him time to speak. I had to kiss his lips. I made sure his shorts came down as well. I got down on my knees and gave him the best head his ass had ever had. Once I felt him tense up, I knew I had his ass. I felt his cum go down my throat and I made sure I swallowed all his seeds. When I was done, I got up and went to the bathroom to brush my teeth. When I came out the bathroom, he was still lying there, looking crazy like he was ready to go to sleep.

"I'll see you downstairs."

"OK, I'm right behind you."

He got up, went to the bathroom and washed his mans off. *Damn, this woman is a beast. She's going to make me get her a ring in the morning just to let her know how serious I am.*

Drinks were being poured downstairs, and everyone was enjoying themselves. He turned on some music, and they began to play spades, arguing more than anything. He and Miracle were in the lead, and Sasha and B were mad because they were losing. The girls looked so drunk, I know they wouldn't be up too long. That way, B and I can get a few games in on 2K and smoke a few more blunts.

"Baby, I'm drunk and sleepy. Walk me upstairs."

"Come on, girl, so I can take you and tuck you in."

"Shut up. Just 'cause I act like a kid sometimes don't mean I am one."

"I know, baby, let me take you upstairs."

"Aye, B, roll them blunts because when I get back downstairs, I'm whooping your ass in 2K."

"Yeah, OK, nigga. You don't want none."

"I'm going to bed, too. I am so tired. I had a long week."

"Aw, my baby tired. You want me to tuck you in?"

"B, I'm a grown-ass woman, just say you want some ass."

"You won't be getting any ass in my spare bedroom."

"Bro, if I want the ass, I'm getting the ass, and she knows this."

They woke up the next day, made breakfast and chilled all day. Iman and Brian said they needed to make a run. Sash and I stayed back at his house and cleaned the kitchen and found something for to make dinner. Sash and I had ribs and chicken on the grill. We had a roast and potatoes in the oven, a pan of mac and cheese, yams, greens, dressing, cornbread, a peach cobbler and a cake in the oven. In the fridge, they had banana pudding, and they made a pasta salad. I had to run to the grocery store while Sasha got everything else together. The guys were going to be surprised when they came back to the house. Sasha and Miracle were having a glass of wine while the food finished cooking.

They had both taken showers and had on comfortable clothing.

"So, sis, you really feeling B, huh?"

"Man, sis, you have no idea. Brian is my soul mate. He told me last night that he wanted us to be together long term. I love that man."

"Aww, pooh, I feel the same way about his rude ass. I can't wait to bare that man's baby and be his wife."

"I can't wait for you to have my godchild, too. Girl, we finally got what we've been wanting."

Iman and B were at the jewelry store. Iman was looking at rings for Miracle and B had just brought Sasha some earrings, a chain, and a Cartier watch. They were glad they finally had some real queens so they could settle down. He thought about how just this year, he and Janay were about to get married. He wondered if he hadn't found out she had cheated, would they still be together? It was still destined for him to meet Miracle, so he wondered what the outcome would have been.

"So, Mani, you really going to propose to Miracle, my nigga?"

"Yeah. I mean, I am not getting any younger. I know she's only twenty-five, but she's the woman I want to spend my life with. I know this happened so quick, but I am going to make it happen soon. I am going to wait until Valentine's Day to propose."

"Yeah, bro, I understand how you feel. I want to give Sasha and me some time."

"Tomorrow, I need you to check on some nigga named Cameron. That's her ex. He's going to be a problem, so I need his ass eliminated. I just have a feeling in my stomach I can't shake."

"I got you, man. Let me put that out there now to our crew. They also said everything out in Atlanta is going well and they moving that product like crazy."

"That's what I'm talking about, my nigga. We can soon retire and live our lives."

Finally picking the right ring, it was a ten-carat white gold ring. It hit me for over twenty thousand, but anything for my baby. This ring was going to be the highlight, and have bitches wishing they were my baby. Every year we were together, for our anniversary, I would upgrade another carat. She meant that much to a nigga. I was willing to move the mountains for her ass if she acted right. I loved her with everything in my soul.

"Nigga, she going to go crazy over that ring."

"Hell yeah, she is. I can't wait to see it on her finger."

"Shit, didn't some Jordans come out yesterday? Let's hit our plug and get them for the girls and us."

"Yeah, you know we got to stay fly, and our girls must be fly, too."

Walking through the mall and walking into Foot Locker, they ran right into that nigga Cameron. He knew today was not going to be a good day, and he was ready for whatever. If that nigga thought he was going to get away with saying some slick shit today, he was wrong. I was not about to play with this kid, not at all. I was the wrong one to keep talking slick to, so he needed to keep it moving.

"So, what's up, nigga? Talk all that shit you were talking while you were at my ex-bitch's house."

"Nigga, I'm going to let you breathe one more day, but don't test me. I am going to see your ass soon."

Cameron chuckled. "Old bitch-ass nigga."

He walked out with his pregnant wife because he didn't want to put her and his unborn in harm's way. He knew he was going to see their asses soon. He could keep acting like he had the best bitch in the world if he wanted to. I knew her bougie, rat ass. Hell, I had made that bitch. He had my leftovers.

"Cam, what was all that about?"

"Stef, don't worry about it, let's go. Stop asking questions."

"Wait, that's her ex? You don't remember Cameron from over off Evanston?"

"That nigga do look familiar."

"Think about it. He got a sister named Erica and Mrs. Beatress is his mom."

"You know what? Yeah, I remember that lame-ass nigga. Put our people on his ass.

"That text been sent. Shit, let's get out of here."

Pulling up to the house, the smell of barbecue was in the air. Neither of them knew who the hell would barbecue in this cold-ass weather, but it smelled good. Walking into the house, they saw the girls setting the table, and they had so much food on the table.

"Who the fuck did you two cook all that food for? We having a party we don't know about or something?"

"Shut up, Mani. Sasha and I felt like cooking."

"I mean, that's cool and all because we're starving, but why so much food, baby?"

"That's how I cook when I feel like cooking."

"Mani, nigga, stop complaining and be lucky. I know I'm lucky they cooked."

"Thank you, baby."

"It looks like you two did some shopping. What's in those bags?" Miracle smiled.

"Your ass always wants a gift."

"We just got the Jordan's that came out yesterday for all of us. You so spoiled."

"Well, go wash your hands and come eat. We're going to stay one more night and go to work from here, baby."

They both went upstairs to Iman's room, hoping Miracle hadn't seen the Zales bag. She was so damn nosy, I bet she had seen it and just hadn't said anything. In due time, we would see. Nothing got passed her or Sasha.

Miracle and Sasha were downstairs having a talk about the Zales bag that was in Iman's hands. They didn't know what it was, but she was happy and ready for whatever he was ready to do.

"Bro, do you think she saw the Zales bag?"

"She didn't miss it. One thing I learned about Miracle is her ass is nosy as hell, and she won't miss shit." B chuckled.

"You're right, bro. She was waiting for us to lie, too."

"Hell yeah, both of them are batshit crazy."

"What did we get ourselves into? They're going to be a handful."

While they were downstairs waiting for the guys to come back down, they drank wine and talked. They had really enjoyed this downtime, but they needed to get back to work. There were moves to be made and money to be made, and chilling with these two, the money wouldn't make itself. Everything smelled good, and they applauded themselves for cooking all this food. There was something about getting in the kitchen and cooking a home-cooked meal. It was beautiful. Both of their mothers always cooked together for holidays.

"Wait, why the fuck is Cam calling my phone?" Miracle asked as she looked at her phone.

"Look, Cam, E is going to come by and get your scale, so can you stop calling me?"

"Bitch, shut the fuck up. Tell that nigga he's a dead nigga when I catch his ass again, and if his boy wants it, he can get it, too. Bitch, watch your back, too. I don't care how much my mama and sister love your bougie ass, I got you for disrespecting me in front of that nigga."

"Yeah, OK, bitch nigga, bring it. You already know I am not scared of your ass, Cam. Tell your mama to get her black dress ready. Out of respect, I'll put the cash up for your funeral, you coward-ass nigga. Come see me. I'll be waiting."

Iman ran downstairs after Sasha came and told them that Miracle was arguing with Cam on the phone. When Iman got down there, she had already hung up.

"Miracle, why the fuck you answer the phone?"

"Iman, I was just telling him that Erica was coming to get his stuff so he could stop calling me."

"Call and get your number changed now. I ran into that nigga in the mall. Aye, B, tell them niggas to find that nigga tonight and bring me his head. I won't tolerate the disrespect, and neither will the girls. Fuck this nigga thought."

Miracle walked away and went upstairs, and when she came back down, she was dressed in black jeans, a black turtleneck and black Timbs with her gun on her hip and one behind her back. B and I looked up like, *what the fuck, this girl has lost her fucking mind.* She came downstairs like she was going to war. She was crazy as hell. Sasha went upstairs and came back dressed as well. B and I started chuckling. This was too much for us. These chicks were crazy as hell. I had never seen any shit like this before.

"Where you going, girl? If you don't sit down somewhere."

"I'm a grown-ass woman. I'm about to go get this nigga."

"Girl, if you don't sit down, I know something."

Funny thing is, he knew I wouldn't lay low. That nigga knew I knew exactly where he was. Cam knew he couldn't hide from me because he just couldn't let go. If he thought I wouldn't move on, he had another thing coming. I was coming for his head, and I wouldn't lay low until I got his ass.

"If you two thugs don't sit the fuck down. We got this."

"Nigga, either get your brown-skinned ass up and go get dressed, you and B, or we leave you here. It's time you met the savage in me, so what is it going to be, baby?"

"Let's go get dressed, man. These girls tripping."

"OK, man."

B looked at Sasha. He couldn't believe how innocent she had pretended to be all this time. She was really a thug. Maybe she was just riding with her girl. One thing I knew, when this was all over, she had some explaining to do.

Chapter Ten

Trouble in paradise

B and I got dressed quickly and came back downstairs. The girls were already in my truck waiting. She was in the driver seat, and Sasha was in the back seat. We got in the truck, and I just looked at her and chuckled, thinking, *damn, baby girl has some savage in her ass*. We took off, going towards the hood. We rode past a couple of blocks, but she didn't see him out there. She looked like she was getting more pissed than she already was before leaving the house.

"Come on, baby, let's just go home. You know that nigga is not going to surface after calling you, acting crazy."

"One thing you don't know is, Cameron is not scared of shit. Trust me, he's in the hood, he just thinks I'll calm down some. He's not going to run; he's going to continue his business like he didn't just fuck up. He thinks his shit don't stank."

"Well, you know the man, sis, so let's go. I'm ready to get rid of his ass once and for all."

Iman sat back, and he finally sat up once he realized they were on Evanston. Iman turned around to look at B and Sasha. Sasha put her black Tom Ford glasses on, pulled her Glock out and put a bullet in the chamber. We did the same thing as we stopped in front of a spot. She got out to knock on the door, and some nigga answered. She let loose on his ass and turned away and said something, but all I could hear was, "Cap." She got back in the truck, and we left. I had so many damn questions. B and I just sat there looking at each other like, *who the fuck is Cap?* She knew he was waiting for an answer, and I knew she wasn't going to explain anytime soon. Sasha and Miracle's phone were going off, back to back.

The next house she pulled up to was right down the street from the house she had just gone in. She got out and told Sasha to stay put, and the look she gave me told me she had this. So, we sat back to see what was next. This was some crazy shit going on. She went to knock on the door, and lo and behold, Mrs. Beatress came to the door. The look on her face told me she already knew whatever Cam had done wasn't nice. Whenever Miracle was dressed like that, it wasn't nice, which led me to believe these two had been doing this shit. He must have made her mad before, causing her to come out of character and act like a savage, but she still needed to explain who Cap was. She gave Mrs. Beatress a hug and an envelope; it must have been cash.

"My nigga, do you see this shit? I swear they got some explaining to do."

"Yeah, they some straight savages, man."

"You don't remember hearing the name Cap a few years ago?"

"Yeah, but I know damn well Miracle is not who they were talking about. I hope not. If so, that girl is something else, and I am going to have to tame her ass quick."

"If that's her, she likes to bust her guns. I heard about plenty of niggas she put down in the hood."

Getting back in the truck, she pulled off. I noticed she was getting on the freeway and her nor Sasha said a word; they were both crying. Their facial expressions showed guilt more than anything. I didn't want to say anything until we got back to the house because this shit needed to be discussed.

"Aye, Sasha, text our employees and tell them they're off for the rest of the week. I will deposit not only the bonus check but another check for being off."

"OK! Sending that out now."

"Shit is about to get ugly. I need to stop by my house. I won't be staying home, so can I stay at your house until this shit is over?"

"Yeah, you don't have to ask."

"I will be paying his wife a visit. He knows he fucked up."

"Can you calm down, please, and take it one day at a time."

"I am the infamous Cap, I won't calm down. One thing I don't play about is disrespect."

"Wait, did you just say you're Cap?"

"Yeah, I did. Is that a problem or something?"

"The problem is, you never once mentioned this to me."

"I try to keep that part of my life quiet. I have changed. I'm not that person anymore."

"Yeah, OK. Next time, be more upfront about what you have going on."

"Upfront? What part of Cap is in the past don't you understand? Cam knows I don't do threats. I don't play. He tried that shit when we broke up, and I shot his ass at his mama's house, then sent her a check to cover her expenses."

"So, what you got to do with this shit, Sasha?"

"B, don't start. That's my best friend, my sister. When she rides, I ride, too. We've been this way all our lives."

"See, Cam made me, Miracle and E this way. He wanted us to be able to defend ourselves whenever some shit happened."

"Well, we not leaving Iman's house, either. We all in this shit together."

"Sash, do you need to go home?"

"Nope, you know I got shit at your place."

Pulling up to my house, we ran in and ran right back out because Cam was going to show up here and we didn't want to be caught. Things could either go my way, and he comes out of hiding, or everybody he thought he loved, besides his mom and E, were going to be touched.

"Say, bro, I can't believe this shit here. I need a fucking shot. Fuck that, the whole damn bottle."

"I'm about to round the troops up and tell them to be on the lookout and close down the spots until further notice."

"I was just about to tell you that, but you ten steps ahead of me."

Miracle and Sasha ran out the house, and they both had two duffle bags. I didn't know what kind of shit they were into. I thought I had a nice angel with a feisty attitude, but hell, I had a thug. They got back into the car, and I noticed Miracle drove past my house. I didn't know where we were going, but I was riding either way. She wouldn't be out here alone.

Pulling up at their boutique, Miracle and Sash pulled the shutters down. It looked like they were in Florida, getting ready for a hurricane. When we pulled back up to my house and got inside, the girls went to change, and B and I were taking shots.

"Man, what the fuck happened today, nigga?"

"Man, I don't know, but I know we have to get to the bottom of this."

Miracle yelled downstairs, "Iman, B, come up here for a minute."

"Nigga, I am taking this bottle. This girl crazy as hell and Sasha just riding along."

B chuckled. "Man, I'm sleeping with one eye open."

"What's up, Miracle? What you need, thug?"

"I need to put our money in a safe. Do you have room?"

"OK, wait a fucking minute. Start talking right fucking now."

85

She looked at Sasha. "OK, look, when I was with Cam, he was doing his thang in the streets. We had been going out since our ninth-grade year. Sasha and I had grown up together since we stayed in the Warren and Connors projects. When we met Erica in ninth grade, me, E and Sasha became cool. Since I was Cam's girl and E was his sister, he made sure he taught us how to survive. He taught us how to cook up, he taught us everything. This is not the first time I've had to do this to Cam. Two years ago, he hid that he was married. I found out his own mama and sister didn't even know. I was walking around, thinking I was his woman and I was nothing.

"I went to his spot, shot his car up and went home to wait for him. From that day forward, we were off and on. I wasn't going to let go, but I was fed up and decided to leave him six months ago. He tried me once again and told me his wife was pregnant and tried to front on me. Well, this time, I caught him coming out his mama's house and shot his ass up. I'm trained to shoot, but I didn't want to kill him. I just wanted to remind him of what he had created: a savage at heart. I told him the next time I had to come after him, he was dead, and I meant that on everything I love."

"Let's go eat, please. I am hungry."

"You stay hungry, Mani."

Making it downstairs, we all grabbed our plates and started eating. Miracle jumped up and ran into the spare bathroom in the hall. I looked at Sasha, thinking maybe she knew what was going on, but she hunched her shoulders without me having to say anything. She got up to go check on her because something wasn't right.

"Best friend, are you OK?" Sasha asked, knocking on the door.

She came out, wiping her mouth. "Yeah, girl, I don't know why I'm throwing up. I must have eaten something that didn't agree with me."

Miracle and Sasha came out the bathroom, looking crazy as usual. These two had been something else all damn day. I needed to smoke, and I needed a drink. They were going to be the death of us. "You OK, baby?"

"Yeah, I think I'm going to go take a bath and lay down for a bit. I'm not feeling too good. Something didn't agree with my stomach."

"OK, baby, I'll be up to check on you in a few."

Giving him a kiss, I headed upstairs, stripped out my clothes and turned on my music to Tamar's CD. I loved this CD. I ran my bath water while thinking, *I know damn well I'm not pregnant.* My period was supposed to start yesterday, but it hadn't. I couldn't be pregnant so soon. What if he didn't want kids?

Getting into the bathtub, the water felt so damn good. I could stay in here all night. I loved this house, and I loved him even more. I just hoped we were not moving too damn fast. Sasha, Iman, and B cleaned up the kitchen and put the food away.

"Bro, go check on Sis and make sure she's OK."

"Yeah, let me go check on my woman."

Going upstairs, I found her in the tub, looking so beautiful. I took off my clothes and got in behind her. I didn't even speak any words, I just kissed her neck to reassure her everything would be OK. It seemed like she had a world of stress on her shoulders. I wanted her to feel my presence and know I was here with her every step of the way.

"How are you feeling, baby?"

"I'm feeling a little better. It must have been something I ate."

"Well, baby, I will take care of you. You being here in my house feels so good. I wish you didn't have to go home."

"Who said I have to go home?"

"Why don't you move in with me?"

"You don't think we're rushing things? I mean, we're still getting to know each other, and you're still finding things out about me you never knew."

"Baby, look, nothing is too soon. God put us together for a reason."

"OK, baby. I will think about it because I don't want us to get sick of each other."

I got out the tub and wrapped a towel around my waist. I wanted to wash her body from head to toe. Once I was done washing her body, I helped her out the tub. I carried her into the room, dried her off and laid her on the bed. I went back to the bathroom and took a shower. While in the shower, it crossed my mind that we hadn't been using condoms at all and she could be pregnant. If she were, I would be so happy to be a father. I couldn't wait to give her a ring and make this relationship solid.

Showering, I couldn't help but think about everything that had happened today. My baby was a thug. When I got out the shower, I went in the room to put on some shorts and a shirt. She was lying in bed, sleeping peacefully. I didn't want to disturb her, so I turned the light off and went back downstairs to smoke with my nigga.

When I got downstairs, B was in the theater room, watching *Belly*. We used to watch this movie all the time when we first started hustling. It taught us how to make sure you keep your circle tight, tighter than a virgin pussy. B was smoking a blunt, and I sat down and started smoking the one I had already rolled. I didn't see Sash, so she must have gone to bed as well. Today was a long-ass day. Hell, I should be tired, we all should, but I needed to unwind and talk to my boy. Something had to be done, so I had to take matters into my own hands to keep her and Sash from getting hurt. I couldn't let that nigga Cam think he got away with the slick shit he had said at the mall, or for calling her, talking slick.

"Look, I have to come up with a plan to end this shit."

"I'm with you on that because shit is getting out of hand. I don't think the girls should handle this."

"I agree, bro. This shit is getting crazy, and my woman nor my sis will be out here in the jungle."

"I'm about to head to bed, bro. I'll see you in the morning."

"All right, bro, goodnight."

We ended our night and climbed into bed with our women. This had been one long day. I didn't know what I was going to do, but something would be done. Right now, I needed to rest my eyes.

Chapter Eleven

Invisible

The week had gone by, and Miracle, me, Sasha and B had looked all over for this nigga Cam. He must have gone into hiding. Something about this situation wasn't sitting right with me. I knew he was somewhere lurking. Somebody must have told him what was up because this nigga hadn't been heard from since he called Miracle a week ago. His wife was missing, too. We had gone by there one day last week. The nigga had left his mom and his sister here in Detroit to handle this shit.

    This morning, B and I were out handling business. We had a meeting with our team to pay them for the week since we had been closed. One thing about us, we took care of business with our people. My other businesses were still running, so I didn't have anything to worry about. I had cameras hooked up to my house where B and I could see almost anything that happened at any of the businesses.

    Miracle and Sasha had gone shopping and to get their nails and toes done. Miracle still hadn't been feeling too well, so she had made a doctor's appointment for some time this week.

It was the first week of February, and I was still holding on to this ring. I had something planned for Miracle, but since all this shit had been going on, B and Sasha had been staying at my place. I enjoyed having my nigga and little sis around, though. I had a big-ass house, so they were good with me. I needed to weigh my options because it was important to keep Miracle and Sasha safe. Miracle and Sasha had told me the reason why Erica didn't get in the middle. Cam had shot and killed her baby daddy a year ago, and ever since, Erica vowed that she was done with Cam. Now I understood exactly what the situation was. Hell, I couldn't blame the girl. I would forget that nigga was my brother, too.

Cam wasn't hiding from Miracle, he was watching her every move and was going to strike when they least expected him to. I didn't give a fuck about my sister. Hell, I had killed her baby daddy, John, because I didn't like his hoe ass. My sister could get it, too, because I knew she was taking Miracle's side. I'd let my mama make it; her old ass was going to die soon anyway. I was one nigga who didn't give a fuck about anybody, only my wife, and if she acted up, I'd stop giving a fuck about her ass, too. I had only married her because she had given me the one thing Miracle's bitch ass didn't want to give me: a son and a daughter. I still remembered the day the bitch shot me, but I planned on getting her ass back.

I wanted that nigga Iman and his right-hand man, B. Those niggas thought I didn't know who they were. I had always looked up to those niggas until they wouldn't put me on back in the day. I didn't know why Miracle didn't remember me telling her about them. Those niggas had grown up right around the corner from us on McKinney. I couldn't stand them because they thought they couldn't be touched, but little did they know, it was time to split their asses up. I didn't give a fuck about Miracle moving on. I didn't want that bitch. I had helped her and Sasha open that damn boutique to get Miracle out my fucking hair.

I had tried time and time again to holler at Sasha so she and Miracle could fall out, but her being the puppet she was, she told Miracle everything, and every time she did, Miracle and I came to blows. Sasha was a bad-ass dark-skinned chick. She had ass for days, big-ass breasts and a small-ass waist. Baby girl was the shit, but she didn't compare to Miracle. The light-skinned bitch was the truth, and she knew it.

I had turned that bitch into a monster. I had Miracle, Sasha and my sister trained to be savages and those bitches were bad as hell. They were nothing to play with. I had niggas in the hood scared of their asses.

My wife kept calling my damn phone, but I was not about to answer her. I was on a mission to get some payback. I kept following Miracle and Sasha around town, but I had yet to find out where that nigga laid his head. I would soon, though. I already knew how to get to Miracle's ass; I was going to kill Iman's ass first. I had been to her house a few times, and she hadn't been staying there, and she wasn't at Sasha's house, so she must be at that nigga's house. Just wait until Valentine's Day, it's going to be bloody.

"Sasha, why does it feel like we are being watched?"

"I feel the same way. I have a feeling something is going to happen. Something's not right."

"Let's hurry up and get through this mall so we can go home. I am tired and want some pickles and ice cream. Let me text Iman and have him pick it up for me so we can go straight home."

Me: Daddy, can you pick me up some pickles and ice cream on the way home, please?

My Husband: Miracle, is there something you want to tell me because you been eating weird lately.

Me: Baby, I am not pregnant if that's what you are thinking, but I'm going to the doctor to find out why I've been sick lately. I love you, daddy, and thank you.

My Husband: I love you too Miracle do sis want anything.

"Sasha, do you want anything brought home?"

"Hell yeah, bring me a Snickers, a Reese's and some cheese puffs."

"Damn, bitch, you hungry."

Me: This girl wants Snickers, Reese's, and some cheese puffs. LOL.

My Husband: Damn, she greedy. OK, I got you. Bye, girl, be safe.

Me: OK, daddy.

Leaving out the mall, waiting for the valet to come, it was cold as hell. They needed to hurry up. I couldn't wait to feel the heated seats on my ass. The truck was coming, so I pulled out a twenty and tipped the valet guy.

"Thank you."

"You're welcome, have a blessed day," the valet guy said.

Making it home, I had to pee so bad. Sasha ran to open the door, and I saw that Iman and B were at the house. Sasha went back out to grab our bags. I was in the bathroom, but I could hear Iman talking about all the bags we had. He always complained about my shopping, but he had given me his black card for personal use.

My doctor's appointment was on February 14th. I couldn't wait to figure out what was wrong with me. Iman said he wouldn't be able to go because he had something to do, so Sash was riding with me. He had been so secretive lately, and something in the pit of my stomach told me I was not going to like the outcome. Plus, Cam had not shown his face.

Sitting in the theater room, watching *227*, I chowed down on my snacks. I didn't know why I had been gaining all this damn weight. If I was pregnant, that meant I had gotten pregnant in Vegas, and I was going to fuck Iman's happy-go-lucky ass up.

I could see Sasha's fat ass in the kitchen, making dinner. It smelled like spaghetti, and she knew that was what I wanted. I had told her earlier to make spaghetti and cheese, fried chicken, garlic bread and a salad. That shit was about to be so good. Iman and B were in the man cave, working out and talking business. Lately, they had stopped talking around Sash and me, so they were up to something. I couldn't take any more surprises, so it better be good. My phone rung as soon as Sash walked out the theater room; it was E.

"Hey, boo, what you up to?"

"Nothing, girl, lounging, watching TV. What is my godbaby doing?"

"Girl, she's bad as hell. I wish you would come get her ass."

"I will when all this shit is over with, sis."

"I was just checking on you. How is Sash's ass doing?"

"She's OK, driving me crazy, calling me fat and shit."

"Sis, you are getting fat. Are you pregnant? Mama keeps saying she dreamed of fish."

"Well, mama must see the fish I'm going to feed her dead-ass son to when I catch his ass."

"Bitch, you are crazy as hell. Tell Iman, B and my sis I said hello. I will call you later on this week, bitch. I love you."

"I love you, too, boo. Kiss my baby for me."

Mrs. Beatress was crazy as hell. I swear every time she dreamed of fish, her ass thought one of us was pregnant. All along, it was her sorry-ass son and his wack-ass wife who was pregnant. That nigga had two kids on me with a third one on the way.

Iman and B came upstairs, and Iman kissed my lips.

"Damn, ma, you need to brush your teeth, smelling like pickles."

"Iman, if your ass don't like it, keep your crusty lips to yourself," I pouted.

"Come here, big baby. You know I love you. I was just playing, crybaby."

"I'll be back, baby. I love you."

"Yep, I love you, too." I was still pissed off. His ass gets on my nerves.

I got up and went into the kitchen with my sis while she was putting all the food on the table. We ate dinner at the table every night like a real family. It was something that brought us closer to each other. I felt like I had known B all of my life; that was my brother. I'd slap the shit out of a bitch for fucking with my brother, my BFFs, my man and my godchild, JuJu

Iman was washing dishes, laughing and shaking his head at the stories we told at the table. They didn't know my pops was the man in the streets when I was growing up. You couldn't do shit without him knowing, so my craziness, I got from my parents. I missed them so much. They lived all the way in Chicago. I said I was going to visit them one day when I had time. My daddy had warned me about Cam's ass, and so did my mama.

B, Sasha, and Iman were drinking at the table, talking shit while my fat ass was still eating.

"Baby, bring me my pickles."

"Your ass is pregnant, I swear. Look at the shit you doing."

"If you don't get your brown-skinned ass out my face, I know something. Keep on playing."

"You're my baby. Give me some kisses, chunky cheeks."

"Oh my God, I am not that big. I still look good."

"Yes, baby, you do. Hell, you got more ass than you had when I met your ass. That ass is wide."

"I swear I am going on a diet right after Valentine's Day, so I can eat all the chocolate you're going to buy me. Straight to the gym to get right after Valentine's Day so the jokes can stop or else we're all going to be in here fighting, and I'm going to win."

B held his hands up, and so did Sasha. The only person who didn't hold their hands up was this savage of a man I was in love with. He was crazy as hell, just like me, and was always ready and down for whatever. He was going to have a lot on his hands fucking with me because these hands were something else and nothing to play with.

I used to box in high school. That could have been my career, but hell, I wanted to do something else. I would not have made it. My attitude was too much, and I would have been in jail. The first time a bitch got out of order with me, shit was going down. You couldn't use your hands because they were a weapon and they could send you to jail.

"Baby, these pickles are good as hell. You want some?"

"Keep those sour-ass pickles to yourself. I don't want any of that shit your nasty ass be eating."

"It's not nasty until you try it. I'm trying to tell you. Come to think of it, tomorrow, I need you to pick me up some peanut butter and some more pickles."

"I am done. I am going to smoke in the theater room."

"I am coming, too, daddy. Let's watch a movie." We all went to the theater room, and *Martin* was on, so we watched that. I loved Martin, he was so funny. I had seen all the episodes. My baby rubbed my feet, and from the sounds of things, it sounded like Sasha was in the back, giving my bro head. Iman and I laughed so hard. I swear they were nasty.

"Go to your room. We don't want to hear that, rude ass."

"Well, bitch, close your ears."

"Bitch, I swear you and Bro nasty as fuck."

We kept watching Martin until they got up and left. We enjoyed having this time to ourselves, watching TV. I loved being in his arms. I was so happy with this man.

Chapter Twelve

The Big Bang

It was Valentine's Day, and I was happy as hell. Iman and I had been together for two months now. I was also nervous because today, I would be going to the doctor to see what was going on with me. Waking up and seeing all these gifts and roses surrounding the bed made me happy about today. I loved Iman, and couldn't wait to spend the rest of my life with him. I knew being with me was not easy, but hell, being with Iman was not easy, either.

Getting up, looking at all my gifts, this man had outdone himself. Clothes, shoes, a diamond bracelet with matching earrings and chain, Gucci bags; this man knew I loved gifts. I hadn't gone all out for him because what do you get a man who has everything? I had gotten my baby an Audemars Piguet watch. It had set me back fifty thousand, but anything for my baby. I had also gotten him a few fits and a few pair of shoes. After putting all my gifts in our walk-in closet, I needed to talk to Iman about us moving into a bigger house. If we were going to be together and he wanted me to move in, we needed a bigger house because I needed my own walk-in closet and it needed to be the size of a room itself.

"Sis, are you in here?"

"Yes, boo. I am in the closet, putting my gifts up. Here I come."

"Hey, sis. Happy Valentine's Day."

"Same to you, sis. Did you sleep well? Today is a big day, and we need to get dressed and go to the doctor."

"Well, we're going to get pampered. I was told by my brother to make sure we get the works."

"Wait, what's going on, Sash? I know you keeping something from me, heffa."

"Shit, Miracle, I don't know. All I know is, when I went downstairs, there was a note that said to go shopping, get something nice to wear, and go get pampered. A car will be picking us up at 8:30 PM."

"Oh OK. Well, let me get in the shower. I will meet you downstairs."

"OK, sis, see you in a few. I made breakfast as well, something light, but it's going to fill your fat ass up."

"Get out, Sasha."

Laughing, she walked away. I was so glad to have my best friend here with me. Things had been so fucking crazy lately. Getting up and getting into the shower, I decided to put my hair into a high bun. Going back into the room, I decided on a pair of distressed black jeans, a Burberry polo shirt with matching sneakers, a belt, and purse to match. Putting on my diamond earrings and my Rolex, I was finally ready to go. I went downstairs, and Sasha was cleaning the kitchen. I hit the microwave and found a plate of eggs, grits, bacon, waffles, and toast. I made sure I ate everything on my plate. I was greedy as fuck, and always hungry.

"OK, sis, who's driving today, you or me?"

"Your ass is, Miracle. I'm tired of driving you around."

"Well, let's go, hoe."

Grabbing her things, Sasha looked too cute. She had on blue, distressed jeans, a ripped-up sweater with UGG boots. I grabbed the keys and jumped into Iman's Range. I missed my truck, but it was in my garage. I couldn't wait to step back into it.

Our first stop was the doctor's office. Walking into the clinic, I had been coming here since I was a little girl. I signed in and waited for my name to be called. I got that feeling that we were being watched again.

"Miracle Captains." I heard my name being called.

"Let's go get this over with so we can see what's wrong."

We got up and followed the nurse to the back, she took my vitals, then told me to go to the bathroom and give them a urine sample and the doctor would be right in. I did everything the nurse had instructed me to do while Sasha's ass was sitting in the corner, texting.

"Girl, you supposed to be here with me, but you texting."

"I'm sorry, this my baby texting me, checking on me."

There was a knock on the door and in walked Dr. Rackle. She was one of the best doctors in Michigan. She kept it real and was a family friend to us. I would never let anybody else look in my pussy.

"Hello, Miracle and Sasha. It's been a minute since I've seen you, young ladies. I take it you all are taking care of yourself."

"Yes, Doctor," we said at the same time. "So, can you tell me what's wrong with me? I am gaining weight, and I can barely keep food down at times."

"Well, let me just do an ultrasound. Lay back, Miracle."

Doing what the doctor said, she put some cold-ass gel on my stomach and started to push on my stomach. I wondered why she was smiling, and so was Sasha. Finally, she wiped my stomach off and helped me sit up.

"Well, Ms. Miracle, it looks like you are going to be a mother in eight months. Congrats."

I looked at the doctor and Sasha and started to cry. I couldn't be pregnant. What if he didn't want the baby? Sasha hugged me. She didn't have to say a word, I had already stressed how I felt.

"OK, Miracle, stop and get your meds from the front, and I want to see you here in about another month."

"OK, I will make an appointment up front."

Leaving the doctor office, I wasn't in the mood for anything but sleep. We still went shopping and got pampered, but I wanted to get home. I guessed I would tell Iman at dinner tonight.

By the time we got home, it was seven, and I hadn't heard from Iman all day, which was weird. I knew him and B were together, and Sasha and B had been texting all day. Oh well, let's hurry up and get this over with. I took a shower and got dressed, and looked too damn good in the red bodycon dress I had on. It was eight on the dot when I was done. I decided to leave my baby's gifts here, and he could get them when he got home.

Walking downstairs, Sasha was dressed in a black bodycon dress. She looked so pretty. She had cut her hair into a bob, and I loved it. Walking outside, there was a red Maybach limo waiting for us, and the driver was standing by the door, smiling.

"Ms. Miracle and Ms. Sasha, the car is waiting for you ladies."

We got into the limo, and we were hyped, but Sasha was not herself. Something was bothering her. I had never seen her so quiet. Whatever was on her mind, she hadn't spoken about it.

"Do you know where we're going?"

"Nope, the driver must know. I didn't get any information."

We pulled up to a building, and it was beautiful, something like a downtown loft. I couldn't drink since I was pregnant, but Sasha was throwing them back. She was a little off, but I would get to the bottom of what was going on with her later. The driver let us out, and a red carpet was laid out. The guys stood there in tuxedos with roses, and I was surprised. They looked good. Sasha and I smiled so hard. Tonight was going to be a good night. Walking to the love of my life, I kissed his lips.

"Damn, baby, you look good," he said.

"You look good as well, baby, but can we get out the cold?"

"Yes, my love, follow me."

Walking in, it was so dark, they had to hold our hands. Once we got to a door, Iman said, "Let me talk to you for a minute," while B and Sasha walked in.

"I just want to tell you I love you, baby, and you mean the world to me."

"Aww, I love you, too, baby. Thank you for the gifts. I left yours at home. But, I am starving."

"Come on, greedy. Let me go feed you."

Walking into a dark room threw me off, but once we got inside, the lights came on and everyone yelled, "Surprise!" I was so shocked, and Sasha was smiling so hard. I looked to my left and saw my parents and my big brother Zeke, which instantly made me cry. To my right were Sasha's parents, Mr. and Mrs. Timons, my godparents. Right behind them was Mrs. Beatress, Erica, and my godbaby JuJu. I didn't see Iman, so I turned around, and he was on his knee.

"Baby, I love you so much. I know it hasn't been long since I invaded your life that cold winter day while you were getting coffee. Baby, I am willing to die making sure you want for nothing and that you are well taken care of. Will you please do me the honor of being my wife, Miracle?"

"Oh my God, yes, Iman. I will be your wife." I was crying so hard.

He got up and kissed me, and we made our way around the room. I didn't know how he had done it, but he had gotten all the most important people here, and that meant everything to me. This man was truly my world, my everything, and I couldn't believe I was about to be a mother and a wife at twenty-five.

Sitting down, I decided I would wait until we got home to tell him about the baby. This day was so beautiful, I swear it was, but it was almost time to go.

Outside, sitting across the street was Cameron. He had followed his bitch-ass mama and sister to this building. He saw when Iman and Miracle walked in and knew this was going to be a bloody Valentine's Day they wouldn't forget. This was the night Iman would die, and there was nothing nobody could do.

Everybody had left, and it was just us left. I had put Sasha's and Miracle's parents up in a room for the time being since they were only going to be here for a minute. I never knew she had a brother. I wondered why she never talked about him, but Zeke was cool as hell. He wanted to do some business with B and me.

"You ready to go, baby? I know you tired."

"Hell yeah, my feet are killing me. I am so tired."

Walking out, something didn't feel right. I looked to the left and the right but didn't see anything suspicious. After the girls got in the car, B got in, and I made sure I was the last to get in, and that was when I heard gunshots.

TAT! TAT! TAT! TAT!

The girls were screaming, and B was shooting back. I couldn't feel anything, and everything went black. I prayed God was not taking me away from my baby. I was not ready to die just yet.

"Let me out, B. Please, let me out. Where is Iman?"

"Calm down, sis," Sasha said. "Please think about the baby."

B turned and looked at us. The secret was out, and he broke down crying. He called 911, and I jumped out the car. My man was on the ground, and he had been shot. This had turned out to be the worst night, and it was supposed to be one of the best.

"Iman, please get up, baby. Please don't leave us. Don't leave me. Please get up, I love you. Please."

The ambulance arrived, and they were trying to do their job, but I wouldn't let them. Sasha pulled me away, and they told us they were taking him to St. John's Hospital, and if I wanted to ride, I could. I jumped in the back of the ambulance barefoot, while B and Sasha got back in the limo and followed us.

Arriving at the hospital, they had lost Iman twice. I was losing my mind. I couldn't believe on the happiest day of my life, something like this had happened. Whoever was the cause of this was going to feel my pain if my man didn't make it. I swear I wanted to stay in tonight, but my baby had this big day planned for us. I loved him for that, but I wished he had gone with his gut feeling. Sitting in the lobby shaking, my parents and Sasha's parents had come to the hospital. Even Erica had come. I wasn't saying anything to anyone; all I knew was that my baby better wake up and come home to me.

Everybody knew not to fuck with me because my mind wasn't there. In the corner, Iman's boys were conversing with B, my brother Zeke, my dad and Sasha's dad. I never talked about my brother because we didn't see eye to eye. My mom and everyone around me was trying to comfort me.

"Sis, let the doctor check on the baby."

"Look, I am not going anywhere until my man can walk out of this hospital. Leave me the fuck alone."

Sasha just had to let the cat out the bag, but I knew she was trying to help. My mom and Mrs. Timons looked at me.

My mom looked at me. "Lanay, I know you are hurting, but I am still your mother. You better get it together now."

"You already know how I get, so just let me be because it won't be pretty if you keep fucking with me."

My mother stood up, and it was about to be World War III. Everybody was grabbing us, trying to pull us apart. I was about to rip this bitch a new asshole if she didn't leave me the fuck alone. Just as I was about to walk away, the doctor came out.

"Family of Iman Harris."

I ran to the doctor, and right behind me was Sasha and B. "Yes, doctor, how is my baby?"

"I am so sorry. We tried everything we could, but he didn't make it."

I had blacked out and was on the floor, screaming. "Please, Iman, come back. Please, baby, I need you. We need you.

B and my brother Zeke got me off the ground, trying to comfort me, but I just wanted my man back. This could not be happening, not today of all days. I finally pulled myself together because I was a boss bitch and I had to be strong for my man.

"Doctor, can I please see him one last time?"

"Sure, but don't be long. We have to get him to the morgue."

B and Sasha said, "Do you need us to come with you?"

Erica ran and gave me a hug. "Baby, please be strong for the baby. We love you."

I walked away and followed the doctor. When I got to the room, a cold feeling came over me. I couldn't believe they had taken my baby from me. Looking down at my ring, I couldn't believe it. I walked into the room, and my baby was lying there with holes in his body. I vowed that whoever had done this was going to pay. I sat beside him and held his cold hand.

"Iman, baby, I love you so much. I am trying to be strong, but this is going to be a hard pill to swallow. You never told me I wouldn't have you for a lifetime. I promise I am going to do whatever it takes to help B get whoever did this to you. I was going to tell you tonight that I was pregnant. You were right all along, we have a baby. I won't let your legacy die, baby. Our daughter or son will know everything about the King of Detroit, their father, Iman Juan Harris."

I kissed my husband and walked out with my head held high. I was a boss-ass bitch, and this was far from over.

Walking out the front door of the hospital, I didn't have to say a word to anybody, they just followed me and made sure I got home safe. I went to my and Iman's room and laid down and smelled his pillow. I requested to be left alone. There were enough rooms in this house, so everyone stayed here. B went out to see what was going on, and I applauded him. I knew tomorrow was going to be hard. I had to plan my fiancé's funeral, but tonight, I was going to sleep. I would wake up and try again tomorrow. I laid down, holding my stomach. Our sweet baby would never know his or her father. Lord, how will I go on without him?

Waking up the next morning, I had to relive what was going on. I couldn't believe Iman was gone. I looked up and saw Sasha, Erica, my mom and godmother sitting at the bottom of the bed. I got up and went to take a shower. I wanted to start planning his homegoing.

When I got downstairs, B said, "Good morning, sis, how you feeling?"

I smiled. "Good morning, brother. Let's plan the love of my life's funeral."

B said, "Sis, no need, it's already been done. Iman knew this would happen one day, so he already had everything taken care of. All we have to do is show up tomorrow. It'll be something small, just for us." I cried so hard. I couldn't believe I was saying goodbye to my baby before he became my husband. It was going to be extra hard for me to go on.

Cameron felt extra good about himself. He had finally gotten rid of Iman. Next on his list was B, but for now, seeing Miracle suffer was great, and now him, Stef and his children could live their lives in Atlanta, or so he thought.

The next day came, and it was bittersweet seeing Iman lying in a box. Mrs. Beatress had stayed back at Iman's house to cook for us. Even though I wasn't in the mood, I knew I had to eat for our baby. Iman looked so peaceful lying there, and it was a beautiful service. Saying goodbye was hard, but I knew he was in a better place, and I would feel better when whoever had done this was gone. Getting back to the house, I just wanted to lay down, and that I did. I would never forget the day I had to bury my baby. I thought what we had was a forever thing, but I guess God had other plans for Iman and for me because He had taken him on the most important day of my life. I guess he was with his parents and he could be free and fly like a bird.

Months had gone by, and everybody had gone back home. The only people who were still here were B and Sasha, but I told them they could leave and that I would be OK. I had sold my house and stayed at Iman's house. I wasn't leaving, all our memories were here.

Lying in bed, I started smelling Iman. It seemed like his scent was starting to get stronger, like he was right there with me. I knew damn well I had watched them lower my baby into the ground and he was dead and gone, so my mind had to be playing tricks on me. When I brought it up to B, he always said, "Sis, Bro is always going to be with you. You just smell him because he lived here." So, I chalked it up to me missing him.

I would be delivering our baby girl November 15, 2018. I wish her dad could be here to see her, but I couldn't wait to meet her. I needed another nap, my head hurt thinking about Iman.

October 25, 2018, I was asleep and dreamed that Iman was alive, and he was kissing me, telling me he loved me. I had told him I was pregnant Valentine's Day, and he was happy, rubbing my belly, telling me how happy he was about the baby and that we needed to set a date for the wedding. I woke up and felt hands on my belly. I reached for my gun under my pillow, but when I turned around, I was in for a shock. Iman was lying in bed with me. I screamed so loud, but he just laid there chuckling. B and Sasha came running in the room, and I had passed the fuck out. When I finally woke up, Iman stood over me.

"Girl, get your crazy ass up. Why you on the floor with my baby in your stomach?"

I had so many questions. Sasha was crying so hard, and B was cheesing like his ass had known all along. Let me find out he knew, and it was going to be a problem.

Seeing my wife-to-be torn up like that fucked me up, but it had to be done. See, I knew Miracle was pregnant, and B and I knew Cameron's bitch ass had been following the girls. His mother had reached out to me and B a week before Valentine's Day. I needed his ass to catch me slipping, or so he thought, so I could get his ass before he hurt my fiancée. I was cool with the doctor here, so I had him make it seem like I was dead.

After the funeral they thought they had, the workers brought my ass out the ground, and I flew out to Atlanta. I knew expanding business down there was something good. Cam's bitch ass went right where I needed him to be, and I was going to end his life right there. Don't get me wrong, I didn't want to kill his wife, but I couldn't leave any witnesses, so everybody had to go. I sent his kids to his mama after everything was done. When she saw me at her doorstep with her grandkids, she already knew Cameron was dead, and so was his wife. She decided long ago to cremate his ass, and she had done the same for his wife.

I was just happy to be back home with my family since I heard I was about to be a father. I needed to be around for my seed, and leaving my Miracle wasn't an option. Killing me wasn't an option; I was the one doing the killing. Miracle thought she was a savage, but baby, I was born in the jungle, so the savage was in me. I knew this was going to be hard to explain to Miracle, but I hoped she understood you have to think like a boss in order to be a boss. It took months, but I had ended Miracle's drama. My brother B had told me how little mama was out here pregnant and dropping niggas. She had dropped half of Cam's crew once she found out it was him who had taken me out, and I couldn't be prouder of her.

It was months after I had popped back up from the dead, and Miracle and I had just become parents for the first time. Miracle had given birth to a healthy baby girl named Imani Jenae Harris. She weighed six pounds, five ounces, and she looked just like me with a head full of hair just like her mama. I was happy we were only a month from saying I do, and the baby I had come just in time. I was the happiest man in the world. Miracle and I will have been together for one year on December 15, 2018, and that was the day we were getting married. Miracle was serious when she said she was getting in the gym. Baby girl had gotten all her weight down and looked good.

It was finally my wedding day, December 15, 2018, and even though Iman was alive and well, and I had just had the baby, I could never get Valentine's Day out my head. Had my baby not been thinking and on his toes, he would be dead and gone, and not here, getting ready to say I do and become my husband. Everything that had happened made me realize I was somebody's mother and I never wanted to feel like how I had made Mrs. Beatress feel all these years. I was going to retire Cap today when I said I do and let my husband be the savage because that was what was important.

Looking at my family, I was happy everything had happened the way it had. Now my best friend Sasha was pregnant with B's baby, and I couldn't wait to meet my godson. Somehow, some way, Zeke and Erica had been dating. My godbaby JuJu was still bad, but that was what kids do. My mother and I had overcome our differences, and I had apologized to her for the night at the hospital. Now that I was a mother, I understood that she was just being a mother.

"Sis, are you ready? You look beautiful."

"Hell yeah, as ready as I'm going to be. I thank you, Sash, for being there for me and putting up with my attitude. I am so happy you're my best friend and my sister. I love you, chica."

All my bridesmaids looked so nice in their lilac dresses. I was beautiful in my Armani dress that I had made just for today. Walking down the aisle, seeing Iman at the end, smiling, and everyone in attendance, made me believe in love again. Who knew I would end up with the same man I had cursed out one day in the coffee shop. This man had been everything to me and so much more. I loved my savage, my king, my husband. Everything we had been through was so worth it to me. I would do it all over again just to get to this day and become Mrs. Harris.

I had a feeling all over again like something was about to happen, but I couldn't understand why. We didn't have beef with anybody, so I didn't know why I felt like this. Nobody better mess up my wedding or Cap would come out one last time. Maybe I was just scared but looking into Iman's eyes made me feel so much better. Lord, I loved this man. He was my everything.

"Miracle, baby, are you OK?"

"Yes, baby, I am OK. You look handsome."

"No, baby, you look beautiful standing here. Aye, pastor, can we get this show on the roll? I am ready to kiss my bride."

Everybody started laughing, even the pastor. "Young man, patience. You have a lifetime to spend with this woman."

The pastor started his sermon. "Dearly beloved, we are gathered here together in the presence of God to witness and bless the joining together of Miracle Lanay Captains and Iman Juan Harris in holy marriage. On behalf of both families, I would like to thank you for being here on this special day."

I cried so hard because this was really happening.

"Miracle, baby, thank you for having my first daughter. Thank you for being my queen and for cussing me out that day in the coffee shop. I thank you for being you and loving me. I just want to say I love you."

"Nothing or nobody can compare to Iman Juan Harris. I love everything about you. I love the way you smell, the way you look, and I love how you look at me. I love you for you, baby. They say love conquers all, and baby, that is so true. I found in you my savage, and I thank God on a daily for bringing you into my life, and I thank B and Sasha for hooking us up. Baby, I wouldn't be the woman I am today if it weren't for you. I love you, and I am ready to be all I can be for you.

We said our I dos, and everything was perfect.

The pastor said, "I now pronounce you husband and wife. Here for the first time, we have Mr. and Mrs. Iman Harris. God bless you two. Now, you may kiss your bride, son."

Feeling Iman's lips on me, I heard cameras flashing. Just as we began walking down the aisle, giving everyone hugs and kisses and thanking them, an FBI agent came through the door. Everyone turned around, wondering what they were doing there.

When we got to the door, the FBI agent said, "Are you Iman Harris?"

"Yes, I am. Why do you ask, officer?"

"You're under arrest for the murder of Janay Waters."

To Be Continued . . .

Coming soon
from
Tiffany Gilbert

In The Heart of Detroit:
A Motor City Love Affair
A Novel By
Tiffany Gilbert

Introduction

Let me start by introducing myself, I'm Tayanna Lori Jones. I was born and raised in the heart of Detroit to Marsha and Terry Jones Sr. I have one brother. He is my heart and my soul. His name is Terry Jones Jr., but everyone calls him TJ. I'm twenty-three-years-old. Me and TJ stay together. He is twenty-seven-years-old. He took the responsibility of being my parent when our parents were killed five years ago.

    I have been under his wings since I was eighteen-years-old. Never the less, he took after our father. I guess being a hustler runs through our blood, I must say. I feel like I have to always be the most fly. I am the hottest. *What more can I say?* I'm 5'5". I weigh one hundred and fifty-five pounds. I'm thick in all the right places. I have long jet-black hair and hazel brown eyes. I can honestly say I was born a bad bitch. I'm the mirror image of my mother Marsha.

I don't hang with too many bitches, so the ones that I do hang with are what I call my right hands. We do everything together. Let's see there's Kyra, Shanti, Jazz, and Kianna. Those are my sisters for life, and I wish a bitch would step to any of them. I've been friends with Kyra and Shanti since kindergarten. We go way back to the ponytail wearing days. We later met Jazz and Kianna, who happened to be cousins, when we got to middle school. In my mind, I'm thinking what will my brother think when I tell him me and my girls have been selling weight. We ran the whole Harper side. Shit was going to get real. I would suggest going into business with my brother. It was something like keeping it in the family. Well, let the drama begin. You haven't seen anything yet. Everything and anything can happen in the heart of Detroit.

Chapter One

The Beginning

Damn it was hot outside. I wished Kyra would hurry up and call me if we're going to the mall. I needed to get me something to wear for the night. We're going to hit up the white party at the *Key Club* downtown. I needed to see if TJ would give me some money. I was hoping that he didn't cuss me out. I called him on his cell phone.

"What's up, pooka?" TJ asked when he answered.

"TJ, don't call me that! I'm not fifteen anymore, damn!"

"You don't tell me what to call you. I take care of you. You're my little sister, but I'm not about to argue with you. What the hell do you want? I'm busy."

"Bro, I need some money to go to the mall. I need to go shopping. I have don't have any clothes."

"Girl, stop you're lying. You just went to the mall on Monday. What else could you possibly want? Man, you're killing my pockets. You need a job."

"Man, I don't need a job! You are my job," I said, while laughing. "Just let me get some money please big bro. I love you."

"Man, you know I don't like you going out to the mall by yourself. Who you going with, one of those chicken heads you call friends? However, on the real what's up with Shanti? You know she bad. I think she wants the kid."

"Shanti, don't want your bighead ass. Please stop looking at my girls like that."

"Ok, you say that but I bet you I get her. Watch a player work. Go look in the safe and grab you five thousand. You know the combination number, and lock it back fool. Be safe and don't forget to take your piece with you. I love you, pooka."

"I love you too, and thank you. See you when you get home."

"Ok, I'll holla."

I called Kyra to see what the holdup was. Or else I was gonna have to drive myself to the mall. I hated shopping alone. These bitches always take they time when they know we got somewhere to go. That's one reason why I try to make sure we plan ahead of time because it is always something with these heffas.

"Damn, bitch, what's taking so long are we hitting the mall or else because you know I can't wear nothing outdated to the club tonight," I asked.

"Yeah, damn. Give me time to say hello before you just start going in on me. I just got off the phone with Shanti. I got to pick her up. Kianna and Jazz supposed to meet me at your house in about forty-five minutes."

"I'll be ready. I was just about to get in the shower. I was just waiting for your phone call."

"I'll see you in forty-five minutes be dressed, Tay."

"Ok, bitch, get off my phone so I can see what I'm going to wear. Bye."

Damn, I was hoping that I would see my mystery man at the mall that day. It seemed like every time I went to the mall he was always there. I had to get his name. I knew my girls were going to be all in to. Oh well, I hopped in the shower because just thinking about his ass got my pussy wet as ever. I threw on some brand new Mek jeans, a little shirt I got from the Burberry store, a headband along with a fly ass purse and sneakers. Damn it, if I was a nigga, I would have been trying to hit on my bad ass.

"Tay, Tay," I heard someone yelling.

That must be TJ, I thought to myself.

"Where are you? Are you home, Tay? Where the fuck are you girl?"

Damn that nigga TJ always comes home at the wrong time. I wrapped a towel around me.

"Damn, nigga, why you yelling at the top of your lungs? I was in the shower. Shit, can I wash my ass?" I asked, while shaking my head.

"I thought you were already gone."

"No, bro, I will be leaving in a minute. Kyra, Shanti, Jazz, and Kianna should be on their way. So, what's up? It must be very important if you yelling like that," I stated.

"Yeah, I need you to pick a nigga up something from the mall. Since you going me and my nigga's are also hitting that little white party downtown tonight."

"Damn, can I go somewhere without you and your friends being there?" I asked.

"Oh, that's where you going tonight? We can all roll together. We got a little V.I.P. section reserved," TJ said to satisfy her.

"Ok, I guess so then bro I'll hook you up."

"Here goes another two thousand. That should take care of my fit. Make me look like a million dollars, girl."

"Nigga, don't play. You know I got taste. Who is that ringing the damn doorbell like that?" I asked with an attitude.

"Oh shit, I think that's Meech. I told him and Tony to meet me at the house so we can do a little business. We got some things to handle before we leave tonight."

"I'm about to get dress before they get here, bro. I know I'm going to have to drive." I told him as I walked away.

"Hey, them chicken heads outside."

"Shut up, TJ. Tell them to come in. I'm getting dress."

Damn, my brother was stupid. I tell you it should have been fun having all of us in V.I.P. that night.

I had to put my *A* game on. It was going to be some ballin' ass niggas in the club that. *Maybe I will see my future husband*, I thought to myself. I need to stop. TJ will have a fit. I took a spin in the mirror and thought damn I'm a bad bitch. I sprayed on some new Burberry perfume.

"Tay, hurry the hell up. You're never on time," Kyra said.

"Aye, Kyra, you better stop yelling in my damn house like you're crazy!" TJ said.

"TJ, shut the hell up! You always thinking you running something," Kyra replied.

"What's up, Shanti? You looking really good today," TJ said, trying to shoot his move.

"Thank you, TJ. You look nice yourself," Shanti replied with a smile.

"Damn, bitch, it takes you so long to get dressed. I talked to you an hour ago and you still not ready," Jazz said.

"Girl, bye. I was talking to bighead over there about something. Let's go because you know it's gone be packed," I said.

"Yeah, it is. See you chicken heads later, and Tay don't forget about a brother," TJ reminded me as we walked out the door.

Chapter Two

Somerset Mall

"The fit you have on is fly as hell," Shanti said to me.

"Thanks, bitch. You girls looking fly to, but Shanti what's up with all that blushing you was doing when my brother was talking to you?" I asked.

"TJ is fine as hell, and I been digging on his ass a long time. I just didn't ever say anything because that's your brother. I look at all of us as family, but I'm not going to lie I would hit that."

"Oh my God, you are nasty, Shanti."

Jazz smiled, and said, "Yeah, he is fine."

"Shut up, Jazz!" Shanti yelled.

They all laughed.

"So, where we going today? Which mall we hitting?" Shanti asked.

"I guess Somerset because we need to be up and out. Oh, by the way my bro and his friends going tonight. They got the V.I.P. on lock, so we all gone roll together."

"That's cool. I'm down," Shanti said.

"This my shit, Tay! Turn this up!" Kianna yelled from the backseat.

I said, "Kianna, you sound like a hood rat."

Jazz asked, "Tay, have you talk to Lando? I heard he was kicking it with some bitch name Angel."

"No, I didn't talk to his tired ass," Tay replied.

Lando was cool. I actually thought we were going to be together forever. I mean, he was there when my parents got killed. That was my high school sweetheart, but I could care less about him. He still is trying to kick it with me every now and then, but I am playing his ass. I just hope we don't see his ass tonight because TJ and his boys going to beat his ass if he tries what he tried last time we all went out.

"Let's get in this mall so we can get out of here. It's already six-thirty."

"Aye, Kianna, isn't that Rome right there?" Jazz asked.

Kianna was getting hype, and asked, "Hell yeah that's his ass and who the fuck is that bitch he with?"

Tay put her hand in her bag.

"Oh shit, I'm glad I'm packing 'cause it looks like it's going to be some shit in this mall," Tay stated.

I was going back down memory lane. See Kianna and Rome had been together since the eighth grade. They never had any problems or any drama. Kianna was what you called a bad mixed breed. Kianna was a 5'6" model type. She weighed one hundred and forty-five pounds. Kianna wasn't too small or too big. She had long straight hair that curled up when it got wet. Her mother was black and her father was Italian. She had a big ass and a small waist with big breast.

"Rome, who is this bitch you in the mall with 'cause I swear you just said you were going to sleep. Here you is here in the mall with some musty rat looking bitch.

"Hold up, bitch! Who you calling a bitch?" the woman shouted.

Kianna looked at Rome, and said, "You better get your little hoodrat friend."

"Bitch I'm nothing but his friend, and I won't be too many more bitches," the woman said.

Rome had to calm everything down.

"Kianna, it isn't like that. This Tasha and Tasha this my girl Kianna."

Kianna smacking her lips, and replied, "Umm, whatever Rome. I don't care who she is. What I am trying to figure out is why you with her."

"Damn, Kianna, you been tripping lately. This is my best friend from back in the day in elementary."

"Best friend, Rome! How come I never heard of her? You full of shit!" Kianna shouted.

Tasha looked irritated, and said, "Look, Kianna, I don't want Rome and Rome don't want me. I got a man. I asked him to help me pick out a gift for my fiancée's birthday."

"Yeah ok, Rome. I'll holla at you later," Kianna told him.

"Damn give me a kiss, baby. You all making a scene out here," Rome said.

"I'm good. I'll call you later or something. Enjoy your day."

"Look I got to find TJ something to wear also so let's make this quick."

Heading into the Gucci store, Jazz's cell phone rang. We all looked at each other because we knew it's wasn't anybody but Tray's doggish ass. We didn't understand why Jazz couldn't do any better than Tray's ass. Tray thought that because he took care of her that he could treat her any kind of way. I didn't know how many times he had put his hands on her or cheated on her. Facing the fact that our girl was blind to the fact that Tray wasn't shit, we hoped that one day she would open her eyes. I guess we will never know. All we could do is be there for our girl until she woke the fuck up and left his ass alone. My brother didn't play that shit at all. He would body any nigga that thought he was going to do his little sister wrong. I stood by my girls through thick and thin, and I'll always be one of their shoulders to cry on if they needed me.

Jazz answered the cell phone.

"Tray, what are you talking about? I'm at the mall. I'm not with no other guy. You are really tripping, Tray. You know I love you, and I wouldn't cheat on you. I know you going to be at the club tonight, and I'm going with my girls. Just have faith in me and trust me. Look, Tray, I'll call you back. I'm trying to find something to wear. Ok, I love you and see you later."

"Jazz, why won't you drop his sorry ass. We are tired of seeing you hurt," Kianna said.

"Kianna, I love him. He doesn't mean to hurt me or do the other things he does to me," Jazz replied.

"Yeah ok, Jazz. Stop making excuses for him," Tay said.

She was fed up with Jazz's excuses.

"Tay, I don't need your fucking input. Damn I know how you guys feel, but as my friends can you guys just stand by my side and let me make my own decisions?" Jazz asked.

Tay was getting pissed off.

"Look, bitch, I wasn't about to say anything about you or that fucked up ass relationship you got. I was about to tell you guys that maybe we should take a vacation to clear our minds," Tay replied.

Shanti said, "Ok, Tay, just calm down. Jazz is our girl and we all like sisters. We love each other. There is no need for none of us to get into it over this. We are all better than this."

"Your right, Shanti," Tay replied.

Jazz said, "Yeah you're right for one time in your life."

"Let's get these fits and go. We wasted forty minutes on some bullshit already," Tay stated.

Everyone in unison said, "Hey, Miss Peaches. How are you today?"

"I'm fine now that my favorite girls are here to shop," Miss Peaches replied. "So, what are you girl's looking for today? Wait let me guess the white party tonight. I got some new things in that will look good on you ladies."

"Ok now, Miss Peaches, I also have to find my brother something to wear. Can you help me out with something for him also?" Tay asked.

"Oh yes, honey. You know Miss Peaches dress the finest men in Detroit. Ok, ladies, have a seat right here and let me have Keisha bring me the things I gathered up for my lady bugs."

"Ok, Miss Peaches."

"So Kyra what's up with you and Meech."

"I mean, we kick it every now and then, but let's be honest Meech is what twenty-seven and don't have no kids and no woman. I think something wrong with him," Kyra replied.

"Like he gay or something? Oh hell no. You stupid, Kyra," Kianna said, cracking up.

"How, Kianna? I'm just saying Meech is fine, and he got his shit together."

"Yeah she rite, Kyra," Shanti said.

Kianna looked, and said, "Oh I guess you a man expert now, Shanti. Aren't you single, bitch?"

Defending herself, Shanti asked, "Yeah, but what does that mean? I still know what I want in a man."

"I hear that, Shanti."

"Here comes Miss Peaches and Keisha. I got to tell you guys something about Keisha. I don't trust that bitch. I'm going to have to pop that hoe in her mouth. She talks too much," Jazz said.

"Ok, we will talk later. I'm just here to shop. I don't got time to be dealing with these bitches."

"Hello," Keisha said, speaking to everyone.

Everyone said, "Hey, Keisha!"

"So, I see you guys going to the white party tonight," Keisha stated.

"Yeah we are. Where you going to double-O-seven?" Jazz asked, laughing out loud.

Keisha looked at Jazz, and said, "I don't find that funny, Jazz. You trying to be funny?"

"No, bitch, I was just telling the truth." Jazz said.

"Yeah ok, Jazz, keep trying me," Keisha stated.

"Now girl's come on now. You supposed to be grown, so act like it," Miss Peaches said.

"Jazz, you know Keisha use to be our girl."

"Yeah, that was until I caught her ass with Tray and they both kept lying," Jazz said.

"Ok, Jazz, I told you I didn't try to fuck with him. He tried to fuck with me. I was just having a conversation with him. I'm not fucking him," Keisha replied.

Miss Peaches told the girls, "I wish you all would this drama stop here in my store. You know Miss Peaches don't do drama."

"Ok, Miss Peaches, we sorry."

"Ok, now lady bugs here is some pieces along with shoes and handbags that just came out. Tay, here is some things for your brother as well," Miss Peaches said as she handed the clothes and other things to the ladies.

I was dancing in the store.

"We going to be fly tonight," Tay said. "I think I'm going to get these white Gucci shorts and the Gucci top that hangs off the shoulder I also want the six-inch Gucci heels and the handbag. I think I'll take those white knee boots also with that white halter khaki dress and the white Gucci bag with the G's all over it."

133

"Ok, Tay, is that it for you?" Miss Peaches asked with a smile.

"Yes it is, Miss Peaches. I want those white linen shorts with the white linen shirt for my brother. I also want the white Gucci belt, the white loafers, and give me the hat. Give me the new perfume and cologne also," Tay requested.

"Ok, Tay, your total will be four thousand dollars," Miss Peaches said.

"Ok thank you, Miss Peaches," Tay said as she handed her the money.

"You welcome, baby." Miss Peaches said. Ok, Shanti, what are you getting?"

"I want this all white one piece, these white four-inch heels, and that Gucci bag," Shanti replied.

"Is that all, Miss Lady?"

"Yes, ma'am," Shanti said.

"Ok, your total is twenty-seven hundred dollars," Miss Peaches informed her.

"Thank you, Miss Peaches," Shanti said with a smile.

"You welcome, lady bug," Miss Peaches said, returning her smile. "Kyra, are you done picking out your things?"

"Yes, Miss Peaches. I want these white Gucci jeans, that white lace shirt, and that white shirt that hangs off the shoulder. I also want that white Gucci bra with those open toe platforms along with that small Gucci clutch," Kyra said.

"Your total is five thousand seven hundred and fifty dollars."

"Thank you, Miss Peaches," Kyra also said as she paid her bill.

"You're welcome, Kyra. Jazz, what you getting today?" Miss Peaches asked.

"I want this one piece Gucci with those white heels that has the G's all over them. I want that new Gucci perfume and that new leather clutch."

"Your total is Two thousand dollars," Miss Peaches informed her.

"Thank you, Mrs. Peaches."

"You're welcome, and Jazz make sure you call me tonight so that I can talk to you about what happen today here in the store," Miss Peaches requested.

"Ok, Miss Peaches," Jazz replied.

Kianna said, "I'm ready. Ok Miss Peaches, I want the one piece shorts and I want that new white-on-white pantsuit with the stripes along those leather pumps and the leather handbag."

"Your total is twenty-five hundred dollars."

"Thank you, Miss Peaches," Kianna replied with a smile.

"Your welcome, lady. Ok you girl's be safe tonight, and I'll contact you girls when the new shipment comes out. Ok, lady bugs," Miss Peached said.

"Ok, Miss Peaches, we love you."

"I love you, girls, too."

Chapter Three

The Pre-turn-up Before the Real Party

After the store was empty, Miss Peaches yelled, "Keisha, bring your narrow ass here. What is going on with you guys? I have raised you and them all together. What's this I hear about you talking to Tray?"

"Mama, you know I would never do that to Jazz Jazz just took what she saw and ran with it. She didn't give me time to explain," Keisha replied.

"Well, Keisha, you need to sit down with her. I'm going to get you and her together on Sunday to talk at lunch. I want this shit squashed. Do you hear me?"

"Yes, mama, I do," Keisha said sincerely.

"Now go and get ready to go home to get dressed for that party tonight. I'll close up here."

"Ok, I love you, mama," Keisha said.

"Child, I love you too."

Since the girls were out shopping, TJ, Meech, and Tony were wrapping up their meeting when the other guy's got there. TJ had to know what was going on. He looked at Meech and started in on him.

"So, Meech, what's going on with you and Kyra? She bad man." TJ commented.

"Yeah she is, but she just play too many games. She wants me to chase her young ass. Dog, you know I am not gone chase no woman. Either they want me or they don't," Meech stated with confidence.

"I hear you, dog. Hell what we look like chasing a bitch." TJ said.

Tony said, "Hell yeah 'cause I'm feeling Jazz."

TJ said, "Damn for real, Tony? I've never heard you say that. What she do put a spell on your ass?"

"Yeah, I been having my eye on her lately," Tony commented.

"Damn, Tony, Tay got some cold ass friends. Hell not to be looking at my sister like that but she fine as hell too," TJ said with a smile.

"Hell yeah!" all the guys said in unison.

Knock! Knock!

"That must be Mike, Shawn, Jay, Greg, Quan, Dee, and Tone knocking one my door like they the fucking police," TJ said as she walked towards the door.

TJ knew it couldn't have been nobody else but his friends because Tay had a key and wouldn't be knocking on the like that. Tay wouldn't do that unless she needed help with all her bag. He knew that his sister loved to shop. If she kept on his ass was going to be broke as hell.

TJ yelled, "Hold on, niggas. Damn, I'm coming."

Opening the door, TJ saw that it was his homeboy, Quan.

"What's up, playboy?" TJ asked as he greeted Quan.

Quan dapped TJ, and replied, "Shit, nigga, I can't call it. What's going on?"

Quan dapped the rest of the fellas up, and asked, "What's up, Dee? What's up, Tone? Shit, nigga, I hope everybody's ready for tonight."

Everybody yelled, "Hell yeah!"

Dee said, "It's going to be some fine bitches in the club tonight."

TJ said, "Yeah my sister and her girl's rolling with us, so I'm thinking we can hit Miami Sunday morning and stay for about a week and a half."

Everyone said, "Hell yeah that's cool."

On the way home from the mall they were just having regular small talk with each other about tonight, knowing it was going down tonight. This was a party that happened every year, and everybody who was somebody was going to be there. The girls attended the party every year, and they couldn't wait to get in the club that night.

"Tay, we going to be some bad bitches. I don't think none of them hoes can see us tonight," Jazz said.

"I hope I don't got to pistol whip one of them hoes tonight because you know I am ready," Tay commented.

"Hell yeah, we some bad ass bitches," Jazz said.

"I think we need to sit down with Keisha and squash all this drama. That's Shanti's cousin," Tay said.

"Yeah it is. I mean, the shit was foul," Jazz commented.

"Let's just think about it. Would Keisha really stoop that low?" Tay asked.

Jazz had to really think about it.

"Yeah you right, Tay. She wouldn't."

"I love you bitches. Who da fuck in all these cars at my house? Damn is TJ having a party before we go out?" Tay asked sarcastically.

Jazz being the rat she is said, "Hell I don't know but somebody got that new Bentley."

"Kyra like hell yeah damn must be paid out the ass."

"Come on let's get dressed. It's eight P.M.," Tay said.

Tay walked in the house and the music was so loud. TJ must have lost his damn mind. I mean, you could hear that music from down the street. TJ got on my nerves when he did dumb ass shit like that. He knew how to piss me off. He was always showing off for his homeboys.

"TJ, turn that damn radio down! This isn't no fuckin' party house, nigga." Tay said as she walked in the door.

TJ looked at Tay like she was crazy, and said, "Aye, Tay, stop always getting smart. Last time I checked I pay the bills in this house and take care of your ass."

"Whatever, here go your shit."

"Where my change?" TJ asked as he extended his hand.

"Nigga, you don't have no change," Tay told him.

"Kyra, oh my God look who it is."

TJ looked, and said, "Like who the fuck you talking about because I know you not talking about none of my boys."

"My future husband."

"Who? Speak now or I'm fucking you up."

Tay had to know who he was, and asked, "TJ, who is that?"

"Oh, that's my boy Quan. Come on and let me introduce you." TJ suggested.

"Q, this my sister Tayanna and those are her friends Shanti, Jazz, Kianna, and Kyra."

The girls all said, "Damn hello."

"Yeah what's up ladies?" Quan replied. "Hey, Tayanna, it's nice to meet you."

Tay smiled, and replied, "It's nice to meet you too."

"Are you ok baby girl?" Quan asked.

Tay smiled, and asked, "Yes, Quan, right?"

"Yeah that's my name, shorty." Quan answered.

"My name isn't shorty. It's Tayanna."

"Well, how old are you?" Quan asked.

"I'm twenty-three-years-old, and how old are you?"

"I'm twenty-nine-years-old," Quan answered with a sly grin.

"How come you never said anything to me before when you see me at the mall?" Tay questioned.

"Because I knew I would see you again."

Tay cocked her head to the side, and said, "Oh really."

Quan replied, "Yeah."

"Well, here I am and here you are, so I guess you were right."

TJ intervened, and said, "Hey, nigga, you trying to holla at my sister? She's off limits, nigga."

"I'm grown and can speak for myself, TJ," Tay stated.

"I'm just playing. He cool people. That's my homeboy," TJ said to calm the situation.

"TJ, let me be the judge of that 'cause niggas in the heart of Detroit not shit," Tay stated with a hint of attitude.

"Wow! Little lady that's not me ok," Quan said to her.

"I'll be the judge of that, but for now let's have a drink," Tay suggested.

"Tay, me and the fella's we talking. We thinking about taking a trip to Miami on Friday morning and coming back in a week and a half."

"Oh ok, bro. I get the house to myself, huh?" Tay asked, happily.

"Hell no! Why don't you and the girls come with us. All expenses paid, but just family. You know have some fun."

Tay looked at her girls, and said, "Hell yeah! You girls down."

They all replied, "Hell yeah!"

TJ looked over at Shanti and wanted to speak to her because of what he was feeling that needed to be said. He didn't want to waste another day or another hour without letting her know what he was feeling. He felt like she could be the one for him to help change him and slow him down. He was getting too deep into the streets and he needed that leading lady in his life.

"Hey, Shanti, come here for a minute," TJ requested.

Shanti blushed, and asked, "What's up, TJ?"

"Look, little mama, I been noticing you and I want to holla at you. Are you single?" TJ asked with a sense of curiosity.

"Yeah, TJ, I'm single. I been noticing you too."

TJ said, "That's what's up. Let's hook up to talk and chill to see what we have in common."

Shanti asked, "Ok that will be fine, so when is good for you?"

"How about tonight after the club? You can stay here tonight. I'm not going to touch you. I just want to talk."

"Ok, I guess, TJ."

"Ok, that's a deal then, Shanti."

Kyra snapped because she was ready to party.

"Damn can you guys come on so we can get dressed?" Kyra asked with a frown.

"Kyra, don't hate 'cause you know if Meech was paying you any attention you would be all in."

"Please, I'm not thinking about Meech's ass," Kyra replied.

Meech heard his name then turned around, and said, "Kyra, you know you love me, girl. Come here give me a kiss."

"Please don't act brand new. You already know what it is with us. You be on some bullshit."

"Yeah ok, Kyra. You going to be my wife one day," Meech stated with confidence.

"So you say, Meech."

TJ was tired of this already.

"Ok enough with all these bullshit love connections. Let's go get dressed for tonight," TJ suggested strongly.

Tay asked, "Damn, Kyra, did you hear what that nigga Meech just told you, girl?"

"Yeah, I heard him. He kind of got my heart beating fast."

"Girl, you need to just talk him and get an understanding," Tay stated.

"Yeah you right. Maybe I will do that when I get some free time, but not tonight, Tay."

"Shanti, girl you and my brother gone hook up. You going to be my sister-in-law," Tay said.

"Shut up, Tay. You so crazy. I promise you are," Shanti replied.

"Hey, Jazz. Why was Tony looking at you like that?"

"I don't know. I was wondering the same thing, girl," Jazz stated.

"Yeah, you need to check into that girl 'cause he was all in."

"Yes, I will talk to him soon," Jazz said with a smile. "Yeah ok, Tay, while you trying to jump off the subject you and ole boy Quan sure was mighty close and talking."

"How did you not know that was your brother's friend?" Shanti asked.

"I don't know. I guess because he doesn't bring everybody around, but what we going to Miami this weekend?"

"Kyra was like I'm happy as hell. We need this vacation for real."

"Yeah we do. Well, I look forward to going to the M.I.A. Let's get dressed so we can show these bitches how bad bitches really look."

Coming soon!